Ben Zombie Novel

Volume One

Jolie du Pré

signed: Jolie du Pré

"Are we the lucky ones? That's a matter of opinion. We are alive, but for how long?"

"Just do it." (Nike)

Precious Monsters Press

Copyright © 2014 by Jolie du Pré

All rights reserved. No part of this book may be reproduced or transmitted in any form or by any means, electronic or mechanical, including photocopying, recording or by any information storage and retrieval system, without written permission from the publisher, except for the inclusion of brief quotations in a review.

Published in the United States of America by Precious Monsters Press
PreciousMonsters.com

Publisher's Note: This is a work of fiction. Names, characters, places, and incidents are a product of the author's imagination. Locales and public names are sometimes used for atmospheric purposes. Any resemblance to actual people, living or dead, or to businesses, companies, events, institutions, or locales is completely coincidental.

Edited by BZHercules.com
Cover art by Danijel Mahovic
Book layout and design by © 2014 BookDesignTemplates.com

Benton: A Zombie Novel, Volume One -- 1st ed.
ISBN 978-0615986036

For Rob, Eve and Aaron.

Are we the lucky ones? That's a matter of opinion. We are alive, but for how long?

–JENNIFER BENTON

1.

SIX WEEK AGO, I NAILED WOOD PLANKS over the sole window in my bedroom, covering the metal blind that's been hanging for at least fourteen years. In the past, a section of the blind got bent so badly, it eventually fell off, leaving an opening. But I was working as fast as a cheetah, nailing those planks. I should have covered the hole, but I didn't. I didn't even think about it.

I crawl to the window and crouch below it. Then, I slowly rise to the hole.

She can't see me. But I can see her.

She's swaying side to side, slowly, like a mental patient in a psych ward, blankly watching my window with those eyes.

They were as green as emeralds, and they were the first things you noticed when she looked at you; not her nose or her mouth, just her eyes.

When I was a kid, when I was upset, all I needed to do was gaze at them, and they soothed me.

As a teenager, I even grew jealous. I wanted *her* eyes, not mine.

Now, they're not green. And the white part around the iris isn't white. No pupils. Just two blue globs.

I can hear her moaning. It's hard to describe, but when they can't see you, I guess they sound like running motors. The sound changes, however, when they do see you. It's a sound you don't want to hear. Trust me.

She scratches the window and, when she does, a bit of her rotted finger falls to the ground. She's missing an arm and both ears. Her gardening clothes were always a bit grungy, but now I barely recognize what's left.

As I rise a little higher, she jerks her head toward me. I fall to my butt and rush to the other side of the room, away from the window, as fast as I can.

As my nerves settle, I tell myself, yet again, to quit looking at my mother.
But I can't help it.

2.

A ZOMBIE IS A REANIMATED CORPSE that feeds on living flesh. Before this all happened, I'd seen them in TV shows or in the movies. But now I know they're real.

The day my mother turned into one is a day that will stay with me for as long as I can survive this. It was six weeks ago, the same day I turned my bedroom into my home.

She's never seen me in my bedroom since she became a zombie. I make sure of that. But my instinct tells me that she knows I'm in here.

Zombies don't sleep. At least the thing that used to be my mother doesn't. It's like they go dormant and then come out of it when something gets their attention.

She's stood in that spot, swaying from side to side, night and day, for weeks and weeks. If she ever breaks the window, if she and the other zombies ever manage to knock down the wood, you'd better believe I'm history without my rifle.

My name is Jennifer Benton. I'm twenty-three and I'm from Waterbank, Illinois. I'm the only person left in the Benton home.

* * *

It happened on a Saturday. My mother was outside, gardening in our vegetable garden, and I was inside, watching the news with my rifle by my side. I had been obsessed with the news for quite some time since the zombie sightings.

Despite everything we had learned about zombies, my mother still didn't approve of guns. Whenever she put her hands on her hips and stared at me with those eyes, I knew I would get a lecture. "Put that damn thing away," she'd yell. It didn't matter that I had tried to tell her, for at least five months earlier since the start of all this, that we needed to be armed.

I can't describe the blood curdling scream that came out of my mother's mouth when she was attacked. At the time, I had never heard anything like it, and it was a sound I hoped I'd never hear again. But the thing is, I have heard it. I've heard it many times in these past six weeks.

On the day it happened, after that God awful scream, I ran outside, rifle in hand, and one of them was on her. I couldn't tell for sure, but I think it was Dan Martin, my neighbor who lived by the park. I'm pretty sure it was him, because the zombie was rail thin and wore a tight black t-shirt and baggy pants. They were dirty and grubby, but I recognized them because Danny thought of himself as a skater boy, and he always wore the same clothing style. I was never into him, but he was a nice-looking guy until he turned into a mess of green blotchy skin with a missing nose.

That's another vision I'll never forget. And the smell; I could smell him as soon as I ran out of the house.

In my bedroom, with that window locked and covered, I can smell my musty armpits and this stuffy air. But I'll take it over dead bodies and rotted skin, any day of the week. I can only imagine what it must smell like outside now that they're all over the place.

Dan had ripped off my mother's arm and proceeded to eat it. There was blood squirting on Dan, on my mother, and on the lawn below. I lifted my rifle, aimed for Dan, and shot his head off. It splattered all over my mother and her vegetables. Yeah, it was gross, and I'm still fucked up over it.

I rushed to my mother, but it was too late. It must have been the gunshot, because three more appeared out of nowhere and jumped on top of her. Before I could shoot them, two more were coming for me.

I ran back into the house and locked the front door. Then I ran into my bedroom, locked my bedroom door, pulled my dresser in front of it, and nailed the wood planks over the window.

I was on automatic. I just did what I needed to do. I expected the zombies to break into my house, but they haven't so far.

3.

MY BEDROOM HAS A BATHROOM, and it has supplies I had gathered over time: water, ammunition, multi-tool knife, food bars, batteries, tampons, medical supplies, matches, flashlight, a radio, and other stuff.

I had stored the wood against my wall and grabbed a hammer from the garage for when I'd need it. My mother had a fit when she saw the wood, so I didn't nail it to my window until it happened.

"You're twenty-three years old. When are you going to look for work? What the hell are you doing with your life?" she would say.

I had graduated with honors from the university. But a degree didn't matter, because I wound up living at home, with no job. To make matters worse, in her eyes, because I was all into the survivalist thing, she pretty much thought I needed therapy.

I'm an only child, and cancer killed my father five years ago. However, if he were alive, he would have supported me. He would have believed my prediction about the pandemic. When birds attacked people in Europe, and then those same people began attacking other people, he would have known something was up. He wouldn't have questioned it when the government quarantined certain areas. He would have believed, as I did, that the problem would eventually come to Waterbank. But he distrusted the government as much as I do, so he would have insisted we rely on nobody but ourselves. After all, he's the one who taught me how to shoot a rifle.

Then, in my neighborhood, it finally happened, and it began with Janet Carlson, followed by the entire Molson family. Government officials showed up, standing around on corners with their big guns. They told us to stay indoors.

Soon we got the 411 on the victims. Janet Carlson got bit. Then every member of the Molson family got bit. In fact, rumor was the Molson family ate one another. Pretty fucked up.

They never told us if Carlson and the Molsons are roaming Waterbank, looking for humans, or if the government shot and killed them.

My mother, however, refused to face reality. She knew there were zombie sightings; she knew what happened to Janet Carlson and the Molsons, but she believed the government would take care of it.

On the day it happened, she said she wanted to sit outside in the sunshine and garden. "I need to get out of this house," were the last words I ever heard from her.

It wasn't the first time she refused to stay in, but nothing had happened the couple of times she had gardened before. The government told us where we could and could not go in Waterbank. If we left our homes, we were restricted to guarded paths.

I never saw zombies on those paths. I realize now, subconsciously, I had convinced myself things might be okay, that it was safe to spend time outside as long as the government protected us. And, on the afternoon it happened, it was such a sunny day, and the sky was so clear and blue; things just had to be all right. But they weren't all right.

After my mother was attacked by zombies, and I locked myself in my room and got the wood up, it all hit me. I curled up into a ball on my closet floor and cried and cried. I left it to use my bathroom, but then I would crawl right back in, balled up, twisting a strand of my long, auburn hair with one hand and grasping my rifle with the other.

A few times, I heard banging on the front door. But the banging was always followed by screaming and growling. Lots of screaming and growling. Even with the closet door closed and my hands over my ears, I could still hear the screaming and the growling.

Sometimes, I'd drift off to sleep, but not for long. Once, I dreamed my mother opened the closet door, and she was standing there, all rotted and smelly, except her eyes were still green.

I stayed curled up in my closet for days. I didn't eat or drink anything. I was content to just sit there, weak and dehydrated. But something told me to get up, to plan my next move, to survive. I could stay in my room, but my supplies won't last forever.

I wish I could talk to someone about losing my mother. I wish I could reach my friends and my relatives. But my mother is dead, and I've been unable to contact my friends and family. I don't even know if they're dead or alive.

What I do know is I've been locked in my bedroom for six weeks. But now I've got a full backpack, I've got my rifle, and I'm ready to get the hell out of here.

4.

MY CAR IS LOCKED IN THE GARAGE, away from zombies and people. It's been over six weeks since I drove it, but it has a full tank of gas, and there's a can of gas in the trunk.

With my backpack thrown over my shoulder and my rifle in hand, I slowly open the door. The first thing that hits me is the smell of zombies and dead bodies. Now it smells way worse than it did when I shot Dan, so bad I feel I'm going to vomit. But what's so weird about it all is that it's sunny, just as sunny as when my mother was killed. It wouldn't seem so weird if it were gray and cloudy.

The sunshine fools you into thinking everything will be okay.

My bedroom window is on the west side of the house. Although my mother is there, she can't see me when I make my escape.

But I hear growling in the distance. So I step back into my house. My heart thumps against my chest. It takes me a few minutes to gather myself. I realize the growls are not near me, at least not near enough for me not to continue with my plan.

I open the door again and step out a bit. I see a zombie on the ground over in my neighbor's yard. It's Tim Morgan's yard. I don't know if it's him or not, and I don't want to know. I rush over to the garage, located in front of me.

My hand is shaking as I stick the key into the side door. I don't see any other zombies, but I keep thinking one of them will jump out from the side of the garage and get me.

That doesn't happen as I get the door open and rush inside. Even though I know there's no zombie in the garage, I still get scared for a second.

I close the side door, open my car door, and rush inside. Then it hits me, what I'm about to do. I'm safe inside my car, but I'm about to open the automatic garage door and hit the street. What if zombies come rushing at my car? What if I can't leave my garage? I push the thoughts out my mind as I start my car and reach for the garage door opener.

I don't think anyone can grip a steering wheel harder than I'm gripping mine now. I look behind me, and I don't see zombies. I rush out the garage and then pull onto the road.

I'm not ready for what I see. The windows of many of the homes are broken, and there's blood on the street and on the lawns.

That's just the beginning. Half-eaten dead bodies lie on the ground. Some are face up, but I don't slow down enough to determine who they are. But I can tell one was a government official. I can tell by the uniform he's wearing. I can also tell one is Mrs. Chester. She's sprawled in the middle of the street. I look away because they've ripped her to pieces. I can tell it's her because of the blue striped housedress she often wore over her obese body.

My stomach is a jumbled mess, and my head is spinning. Then I see one, a zombie, slowing dragging itself up the street, coming right for me.

I hit the gas. As I turn the corner, making skid sounds in my hurry, I see three more!

They're chasing after me, but they can't outrun the car. Then I hear the human screaming. I don't recognize him from the neighborhood. He has a look of extreme fear on his face as he heads for my car. "Help me!" he says, frantically waving his arms.

I consider slowing down just enough for him to jump into the car, but it's too late. Two zombies catch him and drag him down. I keep driving, even faster now.

I reach the ramp for the expressway, and a crowd of zombies stand in the middle of the street, blocking the entrance. My heart stops.

I swerve around the zombies as if they were humans I don't want to hurt. But one rushes for my car and tries to jump on it. As my car speeds down the ramp, the zombie falls to the ground.

I don't look back.

* * *

Entering the expressway, I take a few deep breaths to calm my nerves and to focus. The entrance was always guarded by government officials. If you left Waterbank, you couldn't return, not without proof you weren't bitten. But now, there are no government officials in sight.

Cars pass mine, going faster than the speed limit. I look over at the drivers as they go by. All have determined looks on their faces, as if they know where they're going. One driver glances at me, but then turns his attention back to the road. A sign above me warns that there are zombies in the area.

Then, soon after I see the sign, I see a dead zombie on the road. I dodge it, and then I see another one only seconds later. It's clear that any zombie who wanders onto the expressway won't last long. One passing car appears to be splattered with body fluids.

Tears well in my eyes. I'm not a religious person, but now I want to pray. I wonder if I'll hit a zombie.

Where am I going? What's going to happen to me out here?

* * *

After driving for about thirty minutes, I have to pee. I'm getting close to where The Center is located, an arena where they used to hold major music concerts before this all happened. When I was locked up in my bedroom, I heard on my radio that The Center opened up to survivors. But I also heard the conditions inside The Center are not ideal.

I'd rather keep moving, and I don't want to stop, but I need to. I have to.

I pull over to the side of the expressway and stop my car. I grab my rifle and look ahead, to the sides and behind. No zombies.

I open my car door and dash over to a bush to squat. I notice out here the air doesn't smell as bad as it did back in Waterbank.

Then, right after I'm finished, two young men, seemingly out of nowhere, run over to my car. They're dressed in uniforms from the same fast food restaurant.

"Hey!" I hurry back, but one pushes me down. My knees hit the ground hard. They jump inside my car, throw my backpack out the front passenger window, and take off.

I grab my backpack and hold it tight against my chest. My knees hurt under my jeans, but they're not bleeding. I'm grateful I still have my backpack and my rifle. Again, tears well in my eyes. Why did I leave the keys in the ignition?

Then, I hear screaming. I don't know where it's from, but all I want to do is run. I know The Center is close, close enough for me to get to it on foot. I have no choice but to get there as soon as possible.

I run up a hill, then cross a street. Ahead is the parking garage for The Center. Two guys stand in the entrance.

"Look out!" one says.

I don't look behind me. I just keep running until I reach them.

"Get in here!" One grabs my arm and pulls me inside. Then he shoots the zombie that is coming toward him. I swallow hard. It looks no older than a young male preteen, not as decayed as Dan or my mother was, but he's missing a hand. After the blast, the zombie falls to the ground.

The guy who shot it turns to me. "What the fuck are you doing? You could have been killed."

He's probably not much older than I am, but his stringy hair and pale skin make him look older. A huge gun belt holds his pants on his skinny body. He wears a t-shirt with an eagle and an American flag on the front. I stare at the gap between his two tobacco-stained front teeth. "I'm sorry. My car was stolen."

I look at the other guy. I guess he's around my age also. His facial features are strong and defined. "You were almost toast out there," he says. "I'm Mark."

"I'm Jennifer."

Mark smiles softly and runs his hand through his thick dark hair. For the first time in a long time, I smile too. "This is Gary."

I turn to Gary. "Thanks for shooting the zombie." I offer my hand. He grabs it hard, pulling me into him a little. His eyes scan my body, up then down.

"Think we should let her stay here, Mark?"

I pull away from him.

"Yeah, we've got lots of space, Jen," says Mark.

I glance into the garage, and I see more people, and at least one female.

I hold my rifle close. "If I could just stay the night? Then I'll be on my way."

Gary laughs. "Where the hell are you gonna go? That big gun of yours ain't gonna protect you for long, honey. You'll never make it."

I look Gary in the face. "I'll take my chances." I say that even though I know Gary is right.

"Well, for now, why don't you just come inside?" says Mark. "We took over this garage. There are folks in The Center, but you don't want to go there."

"The Center is fucked," says Gary. "Way too many people."

"Nobody has given us any hassle about our being in the garage," Mark says. "This is the only entrance. Whenever we open it, we make sure it's always guarded. It's dangerous out there, Jen, but you're safe in here."

My name is Jennifer, not Jen. But Mark is a nice guy. Good-looking, too. I don't care if he calls me Jen.

5.

AS I ENTER THE GARAGE, a huge concrete space with more than one level, I see only a few cars. A small group relaxes together in the center of the first floor level. Some sit in chairs at a table. None smile, not that there's anything to smile about these days. None smile except for the girl with the wild red hair, who rushes out of her chair and is heading toward me.

She grabs my hand. "Hey, it's so good to see you. I'm glad you're here." It's as if I'm her long-lost friend.

"Thanks! I'm glad I'm here too."

"I'm Katie."

"Jennifer."

She stares at my backpack. "You got any weed?"

I forgot I was wearing my backpack. I let go of her hand. "No, I don't smoke."

"Okay . . . shit. I wish you did."

Her eyes are blue and wild, as if she's already been smoking. Like everyone else I see here, she looks to be around my age. She wears a floor-length flowered dress and cowboy boots.

"Leave her alone, Katie," says a guy stretched out on a rumpled mess of sleeping bags and blankets. He's got a beard, and he wears glasses. He looks a little older, but not by much. I wonder where all these people came from.

"Come on in," he says. "Have a seat."

Katie returns to her chair and pulls one out for me. "Sit here, Jennifer!" Nobody has the energy this girl has. It's unsettling.

I sit down next to Katie, making sure my backpack and my rifle are close to me on the floor, next to my chair.

"Shoot that thing much?" A girl with short black hair, black clothes, and piercings on her nose and lip sits across from me and glares. In her hand is Poppy Z. Brite's *Lost Souls*.

"Not much, but I had to shoot a zombie who was attacking my mother."

"Did she make it?"

I shake my head.

"Maybe she'll buddy up with my family. They're all zombies now too." She smirks at me and then returns to her book.

Just then, Mark walks over. "You guys meet Jen?"

"Is that your name?" the girl in black asks, looking up from her book.

"Yes, I'm Jennifer."

"You met Gary," Mark says. He points his finger at each person as he introduces them. "This is Katie, Andy, Sara, and that's Eli over there."

They say "hi" back, except I notice that Sara, the girl in black, doesn't. She keeps reading her book, but then she looks up again. "You're seven."

"What?"

"We said we'd only bring ten people in here, and you're seven. Three more people, and that's it. The rest are zombie food."

"But there's so much room here," I say.

Andy, the guy sitting next to her, with the blond hair, laughs. "You been to The Center yet, Einstein?"

"No."

"Well, if you had, you'd see why we don't want a shit-load of people in here."

Sara smirks again and pats Andy on the knee. I assume the two are best buddies.

I take a deep breath and try not to focus on my dry mouth. I want to pull one of my water bottles out of my backpack, but I'm protective about my supplies, and I don't want to share them, not knowing how long I'll be here.

Mark puts his hand on my shoulder. His presence instantly calms my nerves. I look up at him.

"We've closed the door to the garage," Mark says. "Guess you got here just in time. There are sleeping bags over there. The bathroom is in the office over there. We'll all eat in an hour or so."

"Sounds like you guys have it all set up," I say.

"We're pretty organized." Mark is not all muscle, but he's nicely toned in a blue t-shirt and khakis. He walks away, smiling at me again.

6.

ELI, THE GUY WITH THE BEARD AND THE GLASSES, is in the storage garage's office, heating beans on a portable stove. Sara and Katie sit at the table, taking peaches out of cans and placing them in plastic bowls.

Sara stops what she's doing and glares at me. "Go get the plates and stuff."

"Where are they?"

She doesn't answer. I realize it was a stupid question. They're somewhere in the office. Where else could they be in this big, almost empty, garage?

When I get to the office, I see a closet with the door open. The closet is stocked with canned goods and paper products. I'm impressed by how organized everything is. I remove napkins, plates, cups, and plastic utensils. Then I set the plates and everything on the table. Everyone is sitting at the table except for Eli, who is still in the office.

"We're having beans again," says Katie. "I guess we'll all be farting again." Katie giggles. "We've got enough beans to feed an army."

"It was open season on the mart up the street," says Gary. "We grabbed as much as we could before a shit-load of zombies moved in. But if you're nice, maybe we'll let you have meat tomorrow."

"You've got meat?" I ask.

"Yeah, we snagged a fridge and a barbecue from one store, meat from another. We still have power. So the fridge still works. We found a fenced-in spot behind the garage where we can barbecue. Zombies can't get to it."

"That meat is disgusting. I'd rather eat beans," says Sara.

Gary rolls his eyes and chuckles to himself.

"It looks like you guys are pretty settled here," I say.

"We're not staying here," says Andy. "We're moving on as soon as we can."

"Where to?" I ask.

"Yeah, why do we have to leave?" says Katie. She moves her knee up and down fast as she talks. "Everything is fine here."

Andy rolls his eyes. "You really are stupid, aren't you?" Unlike Sara, who seems to love black, Andy wears bright red gym shoes, skinny jeans, and a tight, turquoise t-shirt.

Katie balls a napkin in her hand and throws it at Andy, but it misses him. "No, I'm not stupid."

"We've been through this, Katie," says Mark. "The power will not last forever. We've got to get to a warmer climate."

Eli sticks his head out of the office door. "Beans are ready, guys. Come and get it." Everyone takes a plate and heads over to the office. I follow their lead and grab a plate as well.

A large pot of beans sits on the portable stove. Everyone lines up. Eli is good about separating the portions. It's as if he's had practice dishing out food in the army, or something. Nobody seems to get more beans than anyone else.

We all walk back to the table and take a seat with our beans. The fruit has been separated into seven plastic bowls. There are three water bottles on the table for us to pour water into our plastic cups.

I eat the beans and the peaches. I'm grateful for the food and grateful I don't have to go into my stash of water, food bars, and dehydrated and freeze-dried stuff. The entire time I'm eating, Mark is sitting next to me. Occasionally, his thigh brushes against mine.

"I say we leave by the end of the week, Mark," says Sara. "I'm ready to escape."

"I don't see why we can't do that," says Mark. "The van is ready. Our last step is to stock up on more supplies."

"That van over there?" I ask, pointing at the white one.

"Yeah," says Gary. "It belonged to a family of zombies - mom, dad, and a daughter. They were waiting for humans, I guess." He laughs. "The little girl came at us first. We shot them all. Then we took the van and took off."

"That was a wild day," says Eli.

"How long have you guys been here?" I ask.

"About a month," says Eli. "We'll take our chances and head to Texas."

"Texas?"

"Mark's family owns a ranch."

"I just want out of this garage and out of this damn town," says Sara. "I don't give a fuck where we go."

"Jennifer, you're coming, right?" says Katie. Mark looks at me.

"Of course! I'm coming." It's not like my other options are good. With no car, how far could I get on foot, and what about when night hits? My car could have served as a sleeping place. Now, with no car, where would I sleep?

"If you want to come with us, you have to go with us on a supply run," Sara says. "Everyone has to join the supply run."

Gary, who sits on the other side of me, reaches down and tries to grab my rifle. "No! Please don't touch it," I say.

Andy laughs. "Is that your toy or something?"

"No, but my father gave it to me. It's pretty special to me."

"He taught you how to shoot?" says Gary.

I look Gary in the face. "Yeah. I'm a good shot."

He throws his arms up in the air, mocking me. "Whoa. I don't want to mess with a woman who's a good shot."

"Your rifle will come in handy when we make our run," says Mark. "The more weapons, the better."

* * *

After dinner, we all throw our dirty bowls and utensils and stuff into a large trash bag. I head to the office to use the bathroom, but I take my rifle and my backpack with me. Even though I'm safe inside the garage, I don't feel comfortable without them.

As I enter the office, I notice a worn photo of a man and a woman lying on the floor by a cabinet. I pick it up. I don't know how long it's been on the floor. I wonder if the man in the photo is the person who used to run this place. I wonder if the woman in the photo is his wife, and I wonder if they're still alive.

After I'm done in the bathroom, I open the door and Gary is standing in the office with his hands on his hips. He smiles, but not in a way with which I feel comfortable.

"I'm sorry I touched your gun. I didn't mean to upset you."

I appreciate Gary telling me this, but I don't understand why he had to follow me into the office to do it.

"It's okay. We're all on edge with everything that's happened. Guess I'm just jumpy about everything."

Carrying my backpack with one hand and my rifle with the other, I head for the door. Before I reach it, Gary grabs my arm. "You're awful pretty. You know that?"

My nerves take a nosedive, but I force myself to look at him. "Thanks." I pull away from Gary and rush out to the others.

7.

WHEN THOSE JERKS STOLE MY CAR, they also took my pillow and blankets that I kept in my trunk. Now I'm lying in a sleeping bag given to me by the folks in this garage. I stare at the concrete ceiling, high above me. My backpack and my rifle are close.

The lights are out, except for the lights in the office, left on so we can see our way to the bathroom. I don't know how long the electricity will last. We lost power in Waterbank weeks ago. It can't be much longer until that happens here.

Everyone is in their sleeping bags or lying on blankets, except for Gary. He's sitting at the table, in the darkness, smoking a cigarette. I watch the smoke escape his mouth and swirl around him. I can't stand cigarettes. My father, who died from lung cancer, used to smoke two packs a day.

After what Gary did to me in the office, I'm keeping my eyes on him. Ever since he shot that zombie, I guess he thinks he can do whatever he wants with me.

Katie insisted on laying her sleeping bag alongside mine. She's inside it, but she keeps shifting positions. First, she'll lie face up, then to her side, and then face up again. She's been shifting for about five minutes.

I look over at Mark, sleeping on a blanket across from Katie and me. He looks so peaceful, like he doesn't have a care in the world.

Now Gary is walking toward me. I don't close my eyes. I keep them on him.

Katie sits up and brushes her long, wavy red hair away from her face. "Why don't you stop smoking and go to bed?"

"I am, honey."

He addresses her, but even though it's dark, I can sense he's looking at me. "Good night, Katie," Gary says.

"Good night," says Katie. "Get to bed already."

He stops in his tracks and looks down at me. "Good night, Jennifer."

"Good night." I'm grateful he's sleeping by Mark and not by me and Katie.

* * *

In the middle of the night, I dart up. Every nerve in my body comes alive as I hear the growls coming from outside the garage, followed by an all-too-familiar scream.

"What's happening?" Katie says.

"What the hell is going on?" Mark says. He grabs his gun and flies off his blanket. "Gary! Eli!"

"I'm comin'!" Gary says, gun in hand. Eli, who sleeps the farthest from the garage door, has his rifle. The three run outside.

It's then I see it, shambling into the garage. As the zombie growls, my heartbeat goes into overdrive. It has grey hair and wrinkly skin of the oddest brown. It is only wearing torn, bloody, plaid boxer shorts.

Sara, who sleeps nearest to the garage door, lies frozen in her sleeping bag. The zombie heads right for her. She doesn't scream or move. She just pulls the sleeping bag over her head and disappears into it.

By now, Katie and I are both on our feet. "Oh my God!" Katie says. She grabs me.

"Katie, let go," I say, pulling from her. Then I aim my rifle at the zombie's head and shoot. It falls inches from Sara.

Mark, Eli, and Gary run inside the garage and slide the door closed. Then Gary switches on the lights.

There's zombie matter on Sara's sleeping bag, but Sara still doesn't move.

Gary looks at me. "Goddamn, you shot that son-of-a-bitch?"

"Yes." I run over to Sara, careful not to step on the zombie. "Are you okay?"

She pulls her head out of the sleeping bag. Her eyes well with tears, but she smiles. "I'm okay."

I smile back, and I feel like crying too.

Then Sara rushes out of her sleeping bag, pulls it away from the zombie, and stands up. "Where's the asshole? I told him not to go outside. He told me he wouldn't, but obviously, he waited until I was asleep."

Mark walks over to Sara. "Andy is dead." He looks around at us. "We tried to save him, but they took him."

Katie is standing behind Eli, holding onto his waist. "What are we going to do about the zombie? I don't want it in here. It smells horrible."

"Yeah, yeah, we'll toss the fucker out back," says Gary. "Come give me a hand, Eli."

"No problem," says Eli. "Let's go grab some garbage bags first."

While Eli and Gary dump the zombie, Sara walks to the table and takes a seat in one of the chairs. "I can't believe Andy," she says. "He told me he was getting sick of being cooped up in this place and he just wanted to get some air. He said he'd be careful and take his gun. But I told that idiot to stay indoors."

Mark walks to the table, and Katie and I follow. Katie gives Sara a hug before sitting.

"We found his gun on the ground," says Mark. "When we got outside, two of 'em had him. There was nothing we could do but get back in here as soon as we could."

"He must have made sure he was super quiet," I say. "We didn't hear him leave the garage."

"I wish he had waited to leave with the rest of us," says Mark. "I'm sorry, Sara."

"I'm fine," says Sara. "Andy was a dick."

I put my hand on Sara's shoulder. Despite what she says about Andy, I can tell they were close. She doesn't pull away from me when I touch her. She just continues to stare down at the table.

"Jen, thanks for steppin' up," says Mark. "This whole thing could have gotten a lot worse if it weren't for what you did."

"We're all in this together, right?" I say.

"Right," Mark says, giving me the smile I'm growing to love.

We watch Gary and Eli wrap the dead zombie in plastic bags and carry it to the back door and out the garage.

8.

THERE'S NOT MUCH TO DO when you're stuck inside concrete walls. No Internet. Cellphones don't work. We've got two CB radios. But, basically, we're keeping ourselves busy the way people used to do it before devices.

I've played cards. The last time I played, Sara sat next to me. She was super supportive and laughed at all my jokes.

I've got two books I've stashed in my backpack, but I just don't feel like reading nowadays. I'll lie on my sleeping bag and look up at the ceiling or I'll sleep a lot more than usual. If I were eating as much as I did before this all happened, I'd be heavier, since I'm not moving much now.

Sometimes, Eli will run up and down the aisles for exercise. But nobody else, including me, cares about exercise now.

Today is the day we're all going on our last supply run before moving on. It's been two days since Andy died. I'm nervous about leaving this garage.

* * *

We're right outside the garage and safe inside the van, the one we're taking on the day we move from here. Mark is in the driver's seat. Gary is sitting across from him. Sara and I are sitting behind Mark and Gary, and Eli and Katie are behind Sara and me.

We're all armed. Eli and I have rifles. Everyone else has handguns. Also, we each have shopping bags that we'll fill when we get to the mart.

I turn to look at Katie. She treats her gun as if it were a toy. "Can you please make sure that thing isn't pointed at any of us?"

"Yeah, watch it," Sara says. "I don't want you blowing my fucking head off."

Katie looks at us with those spacey blue eyes. "I'm fine, guys. Stop worrying."

Even though Gary and Mark explained to Katie what to do with her gun, I took it upon myself to take Katie aside as well. But now, I feel like we wasted our efforts.

"Be careful," Eli says.

Katie rolls her eyes.

My heart is pounding and sweat forms on my forehead. I grip my rifle. Fortunately, no zombies are near us, just two farther down, zoned out and swaying like they do.

"Okay, guys; let's roll," says Mark. "Those zombies don't notice us, and I want to keep it that way."

"Yeah, dude, let's do this!" says Gary.

I look out my window, and I notice a dusty red sneaker resting on the curb. I swallow hard, because I know it belonged to Andy. I look at Sara. She doesn't see the shoe.

"When did your mom die?" Sara asks me as the van moves on. Her clothes are black, but her brown eyes are so dark they look black too. Her question is random, but it's one more sign that shows me Sara no longer hates me.

"A couple of months ago."

Sara stops looking at me, rests her head against the headrest, and closes her eyes. "Zombies came into my house and got my family. Got us when we were sleeping." She turns her head and looks at me again. "They know how to open a door, you know? How else could they have gotten into my house?"

I don't know if zombies are smart enough to open doors, but I don't want to argue with Sara. I just want to listen.

"I heard Matthew screaming," she continues. "He was my brother. But I didn't help him. I just ran into my closet and hid. Fucking coward, right?"

I shake my head. "No, I know what it's like to hide in a closet."

"My parents treated me like shit. Matthew was the only one I cared about." Sara balls her fists. "I want to get out of here so fucking bad. I'm so sick of this shit."

I don't know what to say, but I can relate. We all can. I place my hand on Sara's thigh.

Sara looks at me again. "Do you think we can survive this?"

I'm no good at lying, but I do it. "Sure we can." Truth is, I think about dying constantly, but I push those thoughts from my head when they enter it.

"What are you guys talking about?" Katie says, straining her neck to listen.

"Nothing," I say. Sara closes her eyes again, and I look out the window. We've entered the expressway. So far, I see no zombies.

I look at Mark. "How far away is this place?"

"We'll be there in about ten minutes. Zombies may have taken over, but we'll take our chances."

Just as Mark speaks, a zombie dashes onto the road.

"Hit that son-of-a-bitch!" Gary says.

Katie screams as Mark swerves to avoid the zombie, but hits it with the front corner of the van. The zombie crashes into a dividing wall.

"Shit!" says Eli.

"Yeah," Gary says. "You got that fucker!"

"This is madness!" says Sara.

I look at Mark. He doesn't speak as we continue down the expressway. Later, with no further zombies in our way, we exit the road.

"Be ready for anything," Mark says.

The panic I feel deepens as we approach the mart. Zombies shamble in the parking lot, in no particular direction. I wonder how we're supposed to leave the van and get inside without attracting them.

"There's a door around the back," says Mark.

"You've been here before?" I say.

"Yeah," says Gary. "May not be much left, but it's worth a shot."

No zombies come after us. Mark parks at the back entrance and stops the van.

He turns to look at me, Sara, Katie, and Eli. "Take your bags, have your guns ready, and let's go."

We all file out, keeping our eyes peeled for the zombies. When we reach the door, Gary pulls on it. He doesn't have to pull hard. It's already open. We walk inside.

As soon as we get in the door, we're greeted by a guy with a Mohawk who is wearing black leather pants. Behind him, I see other people in the store, staring at us.

"Private property." He points his shotgun at us. "Get the fuck out of here."

"We don't want any trouble," says Mark, pointing his gun. "We just want to get some stuff and go."

"It's ours now," says a blond guy who's built like a bodybuilder, pointing his gun as well. He walks over to the guy with the Mohawk. "We've taken it over."

"Fuck you!" says Gary.

Suddenly, I realize zombies are the least of our problems. "Just let us get some stuff," I say.

"Shut up, bitch," says Mr. Mohawk

"We have just as much right to be here as you," I say. Mark grabs my arm, trying to calm me down.

"What do you guys need?" says the blond.

"Food, medical supplies, water," says Mark. "We're heading south soon. So you don't have to worry about us coming back."

"All right, make it quick," says the blond, putting his gun back in its holster. "And then get the hell out of here."

Thanks to Mark, who I've concluded is the most organized, we each have a grocery list that we prepared before leaving the garage. We'll each carry one bag, leaving our other hand free for weapon use, if needed. Sara's and my job is to gather the medical supplies.

The store is not as ransacked as I thought it would be. Although some shelves are bare or rummaged through, there are still plenty of supplies.

"Can you believe that shit?" says Sara as we walk through the store. "Who do those guys think they are?"

"I know. Let's just get our stuff and go. The sooner we get out of here, the better."

Back at the door are Gary, Mark, Eli, and Katie. The blond, the Mohawk guy, and others in the store are guarding them. I guess they're making sure we leave.

"All right; let's go. Keep your eyes peeled," says Mark. He's the first one to run outside. I can't see him. Is he all right?

"Come on out. Hurry!" I hear him say. We run out, but two zombies are coming for us. Eli shoots them. The zombies fall, but then there are two more. Eli shoots them as well.

Mark, Sara, and I are now in the van. But Eli, Gary, and Katie are still outside. Katie is screaming. She's been screaming ever since Eli starting shooting the zombies.

"Shut up!" Gary says. I hear another gunshot, and then I see more zombies coming toward the van. Gary gets into the van. Then, Eli.

"Come on, Katie!" Mark shouts.

Katie's just standing there, holding her bag and screaming, her gun still in its holster.

Mark and Gary rush outside the van, both shooting at more zombies. Gary grabs Katie and pushes her into the van. Then Gary gets back inside, followed by Mark. But there's a zombie not quite disabled from its gun wounds. It tries to grab Mark's leg, but Mark kicks it off and slams the van door. Then he hits the gas and we escape the zombies that are coming for us.

I turn to look at Katie. "What's the matter with you? Why didn't you run into the van with everyone else?"

Katie doesn't speak. She puts her head in her hands and cries. Eli wraps his arm around Katie. "It's okay. We're safe now."

I don't apologize to Katie. I just stare out the window as we return to the expressway, and I wonder how many zombies will be waiting for us when we get back to the garage.

* * *

The trip back was uneventful. After our escape from the store, we met no zombies on the expressway. There were no zombies waiting for us at the garage, either.

Once we parked the van inside the garage and shuffled out, I apologized to Katie. She was okay, and she hugged me. Katie loves to hug.

* * *

It's evening. Katie, Sara, Eli, and Gary are all playing cards, but Mark is sitting on the floor, drinking one of the beers we got from the store.

I go sit with him. "How ya doin'?"

He looks at me with tired eyes. "I'm okay, I guess."

I put my hand on his leg and, to my surprise, he puts his hand in mine.

"I can't wait to get to Texas," says Mark. "I'm glad you're coming with us."

"Me too. I've never been."

"It's a nice house on about 200 acres."

"You're not worried about zombies being there, are you?"

"I am a little. But I can just picture it in my mind. Quiet. I bet it's still quiet." Mark holds my hand a little tighter. Then he sets down his beer and takes his other hand to my hair and brushes a bit of it away from my face. "You're beautiful, Jen."

I smile, but before I can speak, Gary comes over. "You two gonna join in the card game, or what?"

I grit my teeth. Gary stands there, staring at me.

Mark releases my hand, grabs his beer, and stands up. "Ah . . . yeah, what are you guys playing?" He walks over to the table.

Gary is still staring at me. "You like him?" he says.

"It's none of your business who I like." I get up and walk past Gary, heading for the card game. The entire time I walk, I can feel him staring at my ass.

9.

ABANDONED PEOPLE LIVED ON THE STREETS, or they were the elderly, who were shut off in nursing homes, or they were hermits who refused to cope with other humans. Before our world changed, I never thought I'd be one.

Cancer killed my dad, zombies killed my mother, and my attempts to contact my family and friends had failed.

The day I left my bedroom, I didn't know if I'd survive, or, if I did survive, whom I would meet. But I have a new family now.

We're leaving this garage for good today. We've stocked the van with as many supplies as we could fit. There's enough food and water to last us for at least a month; we're stocked on gasoline and ammunition, and we've got plenty of medical supplies and personal products.

We're taking a chance that Mark's vacation home in Texas is still okay. You would think it would be since, from what I understand, it's practically out in the middle of nowhere. Besides, since there is a lot of land, apparently, the actual home is large and cozy. It sounds great, but Mark hasn't been back there since this all happened.

Honestly, I'm more worried about humans who may have found it than any zombies wandering around it.

But Mark, who never seems to stress much, says we can't worry. We just need to take our chances.

Here in Illinois, when winter arrives, it will be cold, and the power will likely be gone in most areas. At least in Texas, we'll be in a warmer climate, and if Mark's house is still safe, we'll have a place to call home.

In the garage, I'm standing behind the van. Sara is sitting at the table. Eli is in the van, organizing. Gary and Katie are in the storage room.

Mark walks up to me and kisses me on the forehead. He's been flirting with me ever since yesterday, and last night, when he told me, despite everything that's going on, he looks forward to our spending time together in Texas.

His eyes have perked up ever since he started flirting with me. And I'm flirting back, of course. Falling for Mark doesn't scare me. I'm not afraid of what might happen. It gives me something to think about other than the undead and staying alive.

And I'm not afraid of losing Mark to this, either, because if anyone is going to survive, it's Mark. No one calls him the leader, but he may as well be. He's the smartest and the one with the most logical mind. When he decides, no one questions it. He's always so serious and organized. But I loosen him up, and it's nice to see him loosen up.

"We're ready to leave. How are you feeling?" says Mark.

"I feel good; I mean, as good as I can. All I know is, I can't imagine where I'd be without you guys, especially without a car or anything. How are *you* doing?"

"Good, now that you're here." Mark runs his hand through his hair. I notice he does it when he's shy or nervous around me, and it makes me smile. "You came into my life for a reason, I guess."

It does not escape me that Mark said I came into *his* life. Mark is a quiet soul, someone who hides his feelings.

I step closer to Mark. "I'm happy I met you."

Mark looks into my eyes. "Same here." He kisses me on the forehead again. Then, he takes a deep breath and looks around the room. Now he's back in leader and organizer mode.

Eli exits the van and approaches Mark and me. "I think we're pretty much done with packing," says Eli. "Are we ready?"

"Yeah, Gary and Katie are just checking the office to make sure we got everything," says Mark. "I think we're cool."

Gary leaves the office and walks up to Mark. "You want me to drive, bro?"

"No, I'll take the wheel for now." Mark looks at me. "I've got Jen to keep me company."

"Or I can drive and she can keep *me* company," says Gary with that grin.

"No, thanks," I say, and then I walk away to go sit next to Sara over at the table.

* * *

Driving on an expressway is a good way to avoid zombies. I wonder if they can sense the expressway is not the place for them. Probably not, but it sure seems like it.

Right now, I feel about as peaceful as I've ever felt. I'm sitting up front in the passenger seat next to Mark. Mark is in the driver's seat. Behind us,

Gary, Eli, and Katie are sleeping. They're like kids in a car who fall asleep on a long road trip. Sara is reading another book. I don't know how many books she has, but this has to be the third book I've seen her reading since I met her.

Mark turns to smile at me sometimes, but he mainly stares straight ahead, driving while on the look-out for zombies. We've been on the road for about forty-five minutes. Mark doesn't talk, but I'm enjoying the silence and being with him, despite the presence of four other people in the van.

We escaped the garage for good. The only issue was a pileup we met soon after we got on the expressway. I'm not sure how it happened, but there were three cars crashed. Two cars were empty with their front doors open, as if whoever was inside dashed off. The third car was mangled pretty badly. The bodies inside the mangled car appeared dead. There were also two zombies circling the car. We didn't stop to investigate the crash, so I don't know if they ever got inside the car to get at the humans or not.

I look over at Mark again. All I want to do is bask in the quiet and pretend we're all on an innocent road trip. But I have to stop pretending.

"It's going to be a long time before we reach Texas. Do you think we'll make it?"

Mark shrugs his shoulders. I'm stunned.

"I was a person who planned for the future. Now, I just take it one day at a time." He looks at me. "I believe in God, and I believe he'll fix this."

I don't know a lot about Mark or his religious background, but it doesn't surprise me that he's spiritual. Yet, just because he's all into God doesn't mean I have to be. "It's God who got us into this mess in the first place."

Mark shakes his head. "That's not what I believe."

"God didn't save Andy."

Mark isn't rattled. "We don't know God's plans, but that doesn't mean they're evil plans."

"Let's not talk about this. I don't want you to hate me for not being as religious as you."

Mark smiles and grabs my knee. "I could never hate you. I'm not preaching or anything, and I'm not super religious. I just believe in God, that's all."

Sometimes I say things I regret, especially when I'm with someone so composed. "I'm sorry. I know you're not preaching. I suppose some faith could help me now."

"What are you guys talking about?" Katie says, stretching her arms.

I smile. "Nothing, Katie! Go back to sleep."

10.

EVERYONE IS AWAKE IN THE VAN NOW. It's been three hours, and we need to stop. We have our eyes set on an old, white farmhouse sitting next to a cornfield. Mark suggested we go check it out.

We could keep driving, but inching our way to Texas and stopping at places that look safe along the way is the best thing to do. We can cross our fingers and hope for the best by trying to make it there in one long drive, but that wouldn't be wise.

We've made contact with our CB radio. There's a place in Memphis where people are going. But we have no interest in checking it out. We'd rather travel to Texas and make it on our own.

We don't know if the farmhouse is empty or not. If it's occupied, we've decided we'll ask whoever is in the house if we can hang for a bit. If the answer is no, we'll continue on our way.

We're all in agreement that we should knock on the door and wait for someone to answer. But Gary suggests we take it over like we're on some enemy mission. Everyone shoots down the idea.

The farmhouse, with a wraparound porch, is big and historical with peeling white paint. Barns sit near it.

When we approach it, it's then that we see them. Zombies.

"Ah, shit!" says Gary.

"Those are the only ones I see around here," says Mark. "I think we should go for it."

"No! I don't think we should do it," says Sara. "What if there are zombies in the house? Then we'll have to deal with those zombies over there and zombies in the house and that would just be too insane!"

"You're worrying too much," says Gary. "We got this."

"Gary, damn it! This isn't a fucking game," says Sara. "This is fucking serious!"

"Shit, girl! Calm down," says Gary. "It's not my fault your little faggot friend died."

"Back off, man," says Eli.

I give Gary the dirtiest look I've given someone in a while, but all he does is grin at me. "Sara, it's gonna be all right."

Sara just shakes her head and folds her arms.

We've managed to sneak by zombies before by driving slowly and not making much noise. But this time, we're not so lucky.

"Let's get out of here," says Katie. "They're coming!"

Mark ignores Katie and stops the van. He gets out. Gary slides the side door open and leaves as well. I open my door.

"Jennifer!" says Sara.

But I keep moving. My rifle hangs from my shoulder, but I've got a machete in my hand. Eli owns two, and I asked if I could take one. A weapon, other than my rifle, would be an advantage to me. Our bullet supply won't last forever.

Gary has run onto the porch to the front door, but he doesn't bother knocking. Without knowing who or what is inside the house, he kicks open the door like he's a cop or something.

Now, a zombie has made its way up to me. It growls at me, baring yellow teeth, and its smell is overpowering. My heart beats against my chest, but I know it's now or never. I run up to the zombie and plunge the machete into its head. Blood splatters my face and clothes. I get queasy, but I don't vomit. The zombie falls to the ground.

After I kill the zombie, I hear a gunshot. Mark has shot one. "Get out of the van! Come on!" he shouts at Katie and Sara.

I run up to the porch. Soon, Sara and Katie do the same. Katie screams the entire time.

Gary runs off the porch to help Mark and Eli shoot one zombie after the other. One by one, they fall to the ground. After they've shot them all, the guys run to us on the porch and we rush into the house.

* * *

Sara, Katie, and I are in the farmhouse's basement. An old washer and dryer rest against one wall. A rusty blue bicycle rests against another next to antique furniture and dusty barrels. An old doll that looks like someone hasn't played with it in decades sits in a box. The walls are old with chipped paint and the floors are concrete and cracked. Light seeps in from the dirty windows.

This place is so ancient, I assumed zombies lived down here. But Mark, Eli, and Gary checked it out beforehand. They're upstairs, making sure the house is safe from zombies.

I wiped the blood off my face with the shirt I'm wearing. Now I'm even dirtier, but I'm proud of myself for using the machete. I feel confident I could survive on my own if I had to.

"I hear commotion up there," I say. "I wonder if everything is okay. I should go find out."

Sara grabs my arm. "No! Why? Stay down here with us. You don't know what the hell is going on up there."

"I appreciate the guys trying to protect us and all, but I can take care of myself. "

Sara puts her hands on her hips and stomps one beat-up black combat boot on the floor. "You're badass. We get it. But what are you trying to prove? Let them handle it."

"I'm not trying to prove anything. Well, maybe I am. I want to make sure I can take care of myself if I ever have to. What if something happens, and we get separated? What will we do then?"

Sara purses her pierced lips. "Don't leave us down here."

It's then I realize that she needs me. The Sara I know now is a stark contrast from the Sara I first met when I came to the garage. "Okay, I won't."

"I'm gonna need to get a tampon soon," says Katie.

"We sure stuffed enough tampon boxes in the van," says Sara. "I wonder what we'll do when all the tampons in the world are gone. I guess we really will be on the rag."

We laugh, even though the tension is thick.

Katie walks around the basement. "I want to leave. This place is creepy."

"Actually, I hope we can stay here tonight," I say. "It will be nice to sleep in a house for a change."

"What if the owners come back?" says Katie.

I shake my head. "I don't think they're coming back."

Eli opens the basement door. I run up the stairs, followed by Sara and Katie. "Can we get out of here now?"

"Yeah, all clear." Sara and Katie rush over to Gary and Mark.

"You've got blood splattered on your beard," I say to Eli.

"There was one more out there," he says. "I ran out of bullets, so I smashed the heck out of it with a bat."

"Yikes! Your machete did the job for me."

"Yeah, I noticed. Maybe I should take some lessons from you. You're pretty good at it." Eli smiles and I smile back.

Mark approaches us. "There are no zombies in the house. We killed all the ones around the house. We're safe for now."

The men have pulled the drapes across the living room windows. Candles are on the coffee table.

"What if the people come back?" says Katie.

"I told you; I don't think they're going to come back," I say.

"For all we know, those zombies we killed could have been them," says Gary.

"We'll deal with that if we need to," says Mark. "Now, we've got to move stuff out of the van."

"I volunteer to go," I say.

Mark stares at me for a moment. "Okay." It's obvious he knows I'm serious.

"Gary, Eli, you ready?" says Mark.

Eli walks over to the sofa and takes a seat. "I'll stay here with the girls. Jennifer can handle it." Eli winks at me.

* * *

Mark slowly opens the front door. Gary is standing behind him and I'm behind Gary. It's afternoon and it's still light out.

The first thing I see is a dead zombie lying on the porch with its face smashed in. Once again, my stomach gets queasy.

"Don't look at it," says Mark.

"I already did," I say.

Mark turns around. "You okay?"

"Yes, I'm fine."

"Eli beat the crap out of that fucker!" Gary says.

I see zombies scattered on the gravel driveway, all shot with the guns, and also the one I attacked with the machete.

I look around me. Farmland is nothing like Waterbank. It's wide open with fewer people. But the guys took out at least eight zombies, not including the one I destroyed. You just never know.

We rush up to the van, get inside, and close the doors.

"Grab what we need for tonight," says Mark. "I'll stand guard."

Gary grabs the water and I take one of the boxes of food. I also throw a package of tampons into it.

Mark stands outside the van and watches as we run into the house with the supplies. As I run, I'm looking back at him, making sure he's okay. Then we go back for the sleeping bags.

Mark says that even though the house has bedrooms, it's better if we all sleep in the living room together. Once we're done and we're all back in the house, I breathe.

11.

I'M SITTING HERE IN A ROCKING CHAIR. The thing about being in this farmhouse is the quiet. It's as quiet as it was in the garage with its concrete walls.

The furniture in this house is old and antique. Fading flowered wallpaper and framed family photos cover the walls. One photo is of a little girl. She looks into the camera, holding her pet kitten. I wonder if the little girl is still alive.

It's almost midnight, according to the watch I found lying inside a drawer. Everyone is asleep, except for me, sitting here in this rocking chair, staring at three lit candles. So many thoughts are going through my head. Sometimes, I look at Mark, who is tucked inside his sleeping bag.

    I guess I should go to bed. I feel silly staring at the candles, in the darkness, while everyone else is sleeping. I'm feeling a little freaked out now too, even though I know no zombies are in the house.

* * *

    It's early morning. Everyone is still asleep. I leave my sleeping bag and crawl over to a window. Slowly, I pull back one of the curtains. As my eyes search the field, I don't see zombies anywhere. Did we kill them all? I'm not sure why I tell myself that, because I'm a fool if I believe it.

    I walk into the bathroom and use the toilet. I don't look in the bowl, because it's pretty damn gross when you can't flush it. Then I close the lid and brush my teeth with bottled water. I also wipe parts of my body down with it. If there's one thing I miss these days, it's a hot shower.

    I make my way to the kitchen. In a box is some fruit we got when we did our supply run. I grab an apple and savor its taste. I don't know how many more fresh apples I'll get to eat.

    As I'm standing at the sink, in walks Gary. We're all dirty here, but Gary is even grosser. His body odor is mixed with cigarette smell. Plus, it would help if he brushed his teeth once in a while.

"Good morning," Gary says, taking a seat in a kitchen chair.

"Hi. I was just leaving."

"Benton, can we talk? You're always running away from me." Gary lights a cigarette.

I don't say anything. I just stand there and look at the floor.

"I don't know what I did to you, but whatever it is, I'm sorry."

I look at him. I expect to see that grin on his face, but his expression looks sincere.

"It's nothing. I'm just . . . I'm on edge, and I'm not really happy these days. I guess none of us are."

"Well, all we can do is take it one day at a time. We got this far, and we can keep going farther and farther as long as we stick together and use our heads. Your boyfriend will keep us safe."

I feel myself getting mad at Gary again. "Mark is not my boyfriend. He's just a friend."

"Am I your friend?"

I roll my eyes. "Gary, I'm friends with all you guys. Like you said, we all need to stick together so we can survive this."

"Jennifer, look. I'm nothing special. I got no girlfriend. No wife. No kids. I had a good job working on a construction site. Then the damn apocalypse hit." Gary pauses and stares at the wall. "It's always been just me and my old man . . . but I had to shoot him."

"He became a zombie?"

He looks at me. "Yeah, just like your mom. We've got that in common, you know?"

"I left what was once my mother in Waterbank. She would stand outside my bedroom window. She knew I was in there."

"Were you scared?"

"Yeah." I stare at Gary. He still looks sincere. "Can I be honest?"

"What?"

"You're always coming on to me, and I don't like it."

Gary nods his head. "Eli says I shouldn't go around treating pretty girls like meat."

"Eli is right."

"Hey, I'm sorry."

"It's fine. Let's just put everything behind us and start fresh."

Gary takes another puff of his cigarette. "That works for me."

"Okay, well, thanks for talking to me." Gary smiles and nods his head, and I walk back into the living room. I appreciate him talking to me, but the uneasiness I feel around him will take some time to go away.

12.

WE'RE BACK IN THE VAN. This time, Gary is driving and Katie is sitting up front with him. We're out in the middle of nowhere, and yet, we've seen more zombies. A pack of them were lined up along the side of the expressway.

As we drove by them at sixty-five to seventy miles an hour, we were safe. Still, Katie screamed. Gary told her if she wanted to sit up front with him, she'd have to stop screaming.

I'm sitting in the back next to Mark. Sara and Eli are in the middle row of seats. It's the zombie apocalypse, and yet, I'm the happiest I've been in a long time. Mark is holding my hand and, every so often, he'll look at me. There's so much I want to tell him. I look forward to the day when I can get time alone with him, but for now, I cherish being close to him in this van.

We've been traveling for a couple of hours, and now we have to stop to fuel up with one of our gas cans, and we also have to pee.

"Let's just pull over to the side over here," says Eli. "It looks pretty clear."

"Yeah, good idea," says Gary.

"Are there zombies around?" says Katie

"I guess we'll have to find out," says Gary.

I look at Mark. "I wish this trip was over."

"I know. Me too."

Katie, Sara, and I stick together as we leave the van and walk over behind a tree to squat and pee. Then, as we finish up, we hear gunshots. I see a zombie on the ground and I see Eli grabbing his right arm.

We run over to where everyone is.

"Oh my God!" says Katie.

"That damn thing got me," says Eli.

"What? No!" I run up to Eli and look at his arm. Sure enough, he's been bitten.

We stand and stare at Eli in silence.

"Dude, we gotta chop if off," says Gary.

"Hell no!" says Eli, still holding his arm.

"For fuck's sake, Gary," says Sara. "Are you crazy?"

"We've got a shit-load of alcohol," says Gary. "We get you drunk and then remove your arm. Otherwise . . ."

"Yeah, I know," say Eli. "Otherwise, I'll turn into one."

"How soon?" screams Sara.

"A day. Two days," says Mark. "I watched my sister change. It took about two days."

I look at Mark. It's the first I've heard him talk about any of his family members.

Eli walks over to a tree and sits down. "Just leave me here."

"No! We're not leaving you here," says Sara, her hands trembling.

"I can't go with you," says Eli.

"We're not leaving you here!" she screams.

"Okay, Sara, calm down," says Mark. "We'll stay with Eli and camp out here."

Sara nods her head. I can see the tension leave her body. "Thank you," she says to Mark. Then she walks over to Eli and sits down next to him by the tree.

"All right. This is our home for now," says Mark.

"You sure about this?" says Gary in a low voice. "I don't wanna become zombie food."

"Yes, I'm sure," says Mark. "We'll have to keep an eye on him."

13.

WE'RE SITTING AROUND THE FIRE Gary and Mark built. Sara is still over at the tree by Eli.

Outside, at night, is one of the scariest places to be right now.

Eli's breathing is ragged and, often, he'll open and close his eyes. Once, he vomited.

Sara seems oblivious to it. She's poured bottled water on a washcloth and continues to wipe off his face, trying to cool him down.

I feel horrible about what happened to Eli, but I don't dare sleep.

I whisper to Mark, "Who's going to shoot him?"

"We'll worry about that later. We just want to keep him comfortable for now."

I can feel myself getting agitated. "He can turn at any time, you know?"

"Yeah, I know. I'm watching him."

"Yeah, so am I."

Just then, Katie gets up and starts stretching and doing jumping jacks. It's very unsettling to have this girl moving behind me and having to watch someone slowly turn into a zombie at the same time.

"Katie, would you please just sit down?" I say.

"Hey, you need to relax," says Mark.

"I'm sorry." I sigh.

Katie returns to her folding chair. "It's okay. I'm used to you stressed out all the time."

My attitude toward Katie has never been great, and I'm not surprised she senses it. I do feel bad for yelling at her again. With Gary and Mark calmly staring at the fire, and Katie in her usual la la land, it seems I'm the only one worried. Even Sara, who stays by Eli's side, seems less worried than I am.

I lean back in my chair to relax, but I can't even close my eyes.

* * *

It's late at night. The fire is still blazing nicely. Except for the zombie that bit Eli, we're in an area that would be unusual for any zombie activity. There's literally nothing out here, but Eli is getting worse and worse by the minute.

I grab Mark's hand. "I have something to ask you."

"What?" Mark says to me with big, curious eyes.

"We're all fading fast. We'll be asleep before any of us knows it. There's that rope in the van. I think we should tie up Eli with it."

Sara hears me. "What? Are you crazy? He's a human being."

"Sara, please. You're not thinking clearly," I say. "He's getting worse. I don't know if he's going to make it through the night."

Sara gets up and walks over to me as if she's about to kill me. "Who put you in charge? Mark is the leader here, not you."

Mark leaves his chair and puts his arms around Sara to calm her, but she pushes him away.

"We're not going to do it, right?" says Sara. "I mean, what are we here? We love Eli."

I answer before Mark does. "Please be realistic. We don't know how much time he has. If we tie him up, it's only for our own safety."

Sara throws her arms up in the air. "Do whatever you want. I don't even want to be here. I just wish I wasn't here." She turns and runs for the van. At the same time, Gary comes out of the van. Sara bumps against him and keeps on running.

"You agree with me, right?" I say to Mark. "Tying him up is the best thing for us to do?"

"I agree with you, Jen. We'll get the rope."

Eli is ghost white with hollow eyes. His breathing is even more ragged than before.

"Poor Eli," says Katie.

Gary approaches us. "What the hell's wrong with Sara this time?"

"We've decided to tie Eli up, and she's upset about that," I say.

"Dude doesn't look too good, does he?" says Gary.

"No, he doesn't," says Mark. "I'll go get the rope from the van. We don't have much time."

"No, I'll do it," I say. "After all, it was my idea."

* * *

Mark, Katie, Gary, and I are standing over Eli. Sara is in the van, crying. She's refused to come out.

"We're going to tie you up, Eli," says Mark, raising his voice a bit. "It's for the best."

Eli nods his head. He can hear us, but he can barely speak. His wheezing will have transformed into growls after he turns.

We lift up Eli. The whole time, I'm scared he'll turn as we're doing it. We tie him to the tree. I'm glad someone thought to pack a rope.

* * *

Hours have passed. Gary, Katie, and Sara are in the van. Mark and I, surviving on adrenaline, sit in front of the fire, staring at Eli. He's standing and tied to the tree with his head tilted and his eyes closed.

There's a question I've wanted to ask Mark ever since he said he had to shoot his sister. "What happened to your family?"

Mark looks at me. "Zombies cornered us in a store. My father, my mother, and my brother were all attacked. Only my sister Lisa and I made it out of there, but she eventually got bitten."

"I'm so sorry, Mark. My dad died from cancer years ago, but it was my mom who turned into a zombie. Do you ever feel guilty for surviving?"

"Sometimes I do feel guilty I didn't die along with the rest of my family."

I grab Mark's hand, but then Eli fidgets against the tree, which makes both Mark and me jump.

"He's fading fast," says Mark.

"I know. God, I hate this. Where the hell did that zombie come from? It's so peaceful out here."

"Seems to have strayed off a farm or something."

"It will be nice when we get to your ranch."

Mark squeezes my hand. "It will be paradise."

Mark leans over and kisses me on the lips. He keeps them there, and I savor his taste. Then he kisses my nose, and my body tingles.

"What's going on between us?" I whisper.

"I think I'm falling for you." He leans over to kiss me again.

Then, we hear a growl. Eli's eyes are wide open as saliva shoots out of his mouth. He's moving hard against the rope, struggling to get out.

Mark and I dart up from our chairs, and Mark grabs his gun, rushes to Eli, points, and fires. Blood shoots from Eli's head as his body falls forward against the rope.

I didn't know Eli for very long, but we've all become close. Tears fall down my face faster than I expected.

Mark puts his gun back in his holster and hugs me.

"How are we going to survive this?" I say.

Mark doesn't answer. He just hugs me tighter.

* * *

Mark and I buried Eli. We could have waited for everyone to wake up, but we felt it best just to get it over with.

We're back in the van. No one has said much. Gary is driving and both he and Katie are quiet up front. Sara stares at the window with a blank expression on her face.

Mark is asleep, not surprising since we've been up all night. I should be too. I look like shit from the lack of it.

"Are you okay?" I ask Sara.

She doesn't answer. She just continues to gaze at the window.

We don't want to camp outside again. It's much safer to be in a house. However, like before, we'll have to find one that's suitable. Then, we'll have to ask permission, assuming the occupants are still alive.

Are we the lucky ones? That's a matter of opinion. We are alive, but for how long? Mark has it in his mind that his place in Texas is our final refuge. He has faith that the zombie situation will end and humans can get on with life again. When I look into his handsome face, I so want to believe him.

14.

AS I SIT IN THE VAN, I look out my window. I see a river behind the trees. The water sparkles in the sunshine, and it looks so clean and inviting. All I want to do is get out of this van and jump into it.

I look at Mark. He's still sleeping. I look around the van. Everyone is so quiet, and we're all so miserable and dirty. A dip in the river is what this group needs, and I don't think zombies can swim.

"Gary?"

"What?"

"Let's turn around. There's a river back that way. Let's go swimming."

"Hey, yeah! That would be fun!" says Katie.

"You saw a river?" says Gary.

"Yes, let's turn this van around and let's get in the river. I want to get wet. I want to get clean."

Then, Sara comes out of her fog and looks at me. Then she looks at Gary. "Turn this damn thing around. I want to get off."

"Settle down. You chicks are driving me crazy," says Gary.

"Are you going to turn it around or not?" I say.

"Yeah, yeah, I'm turning."

After Gary has parked the van in a secure place, we grab towels and I also bring shampoo.

Out here, I see no zombies; just trees, water, and blue sky. It's nice to think we're safe, but as we leave the van, we all take our weapons. We never go outside without them.

We stare at the river. Sara places her gun on the ground and then she removes her black boots. After that, she removes her black pants, followed by her black shirt. She stands only in red-flowered panties and no bra.

Gary nudges Mark. "Check it out, man!" Mark looks embarrassed and doesn't say anything.

"Sara!" says Katie. But Sara ignores her and removes her panties, throwing them to the ground. Then she runs into the water. She swims out into the river and then just treads water with her back turned to us.

"Well, I'm going in too," I say.

"You gonna take your clothes off?" says Gary.

I roll my eyes. "No, I'm not." I remove my shoes and socks and set them next to my machete. Then I walk into the river until the water is up to my waist. I dunk myself under and I hold my breath as the water soaks through my clothes. When I rise, I feel renewed.

As I push the water through my hair, I see that Sara is no longer treading. She's swimming, farther and farther away.

"Sara!"

She stops swimming and turns around. "What?"

"Where are you going?"

"I just want to be by myself for a while, okay?"

"Okay, no problem."

Sara then does something I don't expect. She smiles at me. I smile back.

Arms circle my waist. "Got you!" says Mark. I turn around and I'm looking right into Mark's eyes. "The water feels good," he says. Mark looks even more handsome with wet hair.

Then we hear Katie scream. We turn our heads, only to find Gary lifting Katie up and then tossing her into the water. No harm. She seems to like it.

As I watch them play, I wish I could cement this moment.

"I want to wash my hair," I say. "Want to wash hair with me?"

Mark grins. "I would love to wash my hair with you, Jen."

I laugh, and Mark and I wade through the water to where our shoes and weapons are so we can retrieve the shampoo. I look over at Sara, who is still in the middle of the river, away from everyone.

"You think she's okay?" says Mark.

"She's fine. She smiled at me."

"Really?"

"Yep."

We walk back into the water. Mark pours shampoo into his hand and then he starts washing my hair with it. I don't expect it, and I try not to beam like the Cheshire Cat. Then I do the same for him.

As we're rinsing our hair, I see a zombie wandering on the other side of the river from where we've parked the van. Katie and Gary are still playing in the water and don't see it. But Sara gives it the finger.

"Come on, Sara. Time to go," screams Mark.

Sara swims back without protest. I'm grateful for that. She walks her naked body out of the water, wraps herself in a towel, and then grabs her boots and her gun.

"What about your clothes?" I ask.

"Leave them here," she says, walking away. "I don't want to see them again."

Gary and Mark stand outside the van while we girls get dressed first.

Once on the van, we grab clean clothes and a plastic bag to throw our wet things in.

"That was fun. I can't believe you got naked, Sara," says Katie, throwing her wet skirt into the bag.

"I don't give a shit who looks at me," says Sara. The smile that she gave me at the river is gone. I'm just glad she was able to get a bit of happiness today.

15.

TO OUR RIGHT IS A MOTEL. An elderly man crouches at the side of a soda machine. He hides his head in his folded arms.

Zombies shamble toward the other side of the machine. They don't know a human is hiding from them, but soon, they will know.

"They're gonna get him!" Katie says.

Gary stops the van, grabs his gun, and gets out. Mark rushes out with his gun as well. I follow with my rifle.

Outside the van, I aim for a zombie. I shoot it and then I shoot two more. Meanwhile, Gary and Mark are shooting.

"Stay there, don't move," screams Mark to the man. The man nods his head and then buries it back into his folded arms.

Eventually, all the zombies are down. We run over to the man. He trembles as we help him up. He must be at least eighty and he's emaciated. As I grab his arm, I can feel his bones.

"Are you all right?" I ask.

"Yes. Thank you. I thought I was a goner."

"Are you with anyone?" Mark asks.

"No. I stay here alone. I've been hiding out, watching the zombies from my window. It was just one or two at first, then more and more."

"Is there anyone else here at this motel?" I ask.

"Yes, but they don't come out. I shouldn't have come out. Everyone is hiding."

"Where's your room?" says Gary.

"Over there."

We walk the man back to his motel room. Inside, we see the room is large, with two full-sized beds that look like they haven't been slept in.

"I'm Bill," says the man. "You folks staying?"

"Bill, my name is Jennifer, and this is Gary and Mark. Our friends, Sara and Katie, are still in our van. Actually, we'd love to stay overnight, if we can. Sure would help us. We're on our way to Texas."

"If you don't mind, Bill," says Mark.

Bill's face lights up. "I don't mind at all. I could use the company. Got any food?"

"Yeah," says Gary. "We got lots of food."

I smile. "Thank you. I'll go get Katie and Sara. They must be worried sick."

Gary and I run back to the van while Mark stays with Bill.

Back at the van, Katie is staring at us, bug-eyed. Sara is still gazing out her window, as if nothing just happened.

"We're sleeping at this motel tonight," says Gary. "We saved the old man, so he said we can stay in his room."

"Really?" says Katie. "Are you sure it's okay for us to join him?"

"Yeah, dude's got a big ass room." Gary points. "It's right over there. Number five."

"So let's grab some food and stuff and bring them to the room," I say. "His name is Bill, and he looks like he hasn't eaten in weeks."

"See, Sara," says Katie. "Everything is going to be all right."

I look at Sara. "You okay?"

She stares out the window and doesn't answer.

"Sara, I said are you okay?"

Sara jerks her head and glares at me. "Yes, I'm fine. I'm fine." She gets up and runs out the van to Bill's motel room.

* * *

As we arrive at Bill's room, he's standing in the doorway. Despite everything that's happening, he looks content.

Katie places her bag on the floor and gives Bill a hug. "Hi, I'm Katie."

"Well, hello there!" Bill says, hugging her back.

Sara is already in the room, sitting in a chair and staring at the floor. We close the motel room door and put the supplies on the top of a dresser.

I look in the bathroom. Bill has placed a pillow and a blanket in the bathtub.

I stick my head out. "You've been sleeping in here, Bill?"

"Yes, I feel safer that way."

Mark pats Bill's back. "We'll set up here and get you something to eat, and no more sleeping in the bathroom for you."

"I'm just so grateful you young people came by to see me."

Katie whispers into my ear, "We can't leave Bill here. We've got to take him with us."

"We'll talk about it later," I say.

Sara is rocking back and forth in her chair, staring at the floor, balling her fist on her lap.

I go over to her and kneel in front of her. "How's it going?"

"What day is it?" she says.

"Um . . . I don't know. I never know what day it is anymore."

"It's Sunday," says Katie. "My diary says it's Sunday."

"When we were swimming, it reminded me of when I used to go to the beach with my brother on Sundays," says Sara. "That used to be our way of taking a break from everything. Just hanging on the beach, you know?"

"Yeah, I know. One of these days, I'll go to the beach again."

Sara's expression changes. "What makes you think you'll ever have the life you used to have? It's over, Jennifer, over."

"Well, it's over for now, but things will get better."

Sara lets out a demonic laugh. "Don't you get it? This is it. We're fucked. Those things have taken over."

"Sara, calm down," says Mark.

"Don't tell me to fucking calm down. I'm tired of people telling me to calm down."

Poor Bill stares at Sara, wondering what the heck is going on.

* * *

The motel room door is double locked. The curtains are closed, blocking all view from the outside. Katie peeks out the curtains and sees two zombies down the road. We remind her that the curtains need to stay closed and to stay away from the window.

We're preparing our food. Bill lies on the bed, watching us. It makes me happy to know we saved him from what could have been a disaster. Sara, however, hasn't left her spot.

"I'm worried about her," whispers Mark.

"Yeah, me too," I say. "Andy's death was hard for her, and losing Eli hasn't helped."

* * *

We're eating our food. Every so often, I notice Bill staring at Sara with a worried look on his face. Gary notices it too.

"Don't mind her," says Gary. "She's just crazy, is all."

Sara gives Gary a stern look, but she doesn't say anything.

"My wife died, and we lost our son before she died," says Bill. "I've been a widow for quite some time. Then zombies drove me and Jim, my neighbor, out of our homes. Luckily for me, Jim owns this motel and put me up in this room. Used to share it with two other people, but, they left and never came back."

"What about Jim?" says Katie. "Is Jim alive?"

Bill looks at Katie and doesn't say anything at first, but then he speaks. "The last time I saw Jim, he was a zombie. Saw him outside my window. He grabbed someone, but I stopped looking after that." Bill sets his empty plate down. "I was going to knock on doors and beg for food. But you see what happened. I'm all out. There's nothing left."

"Then it's a good thing we came by," I say. "Especially because the other people in this motel are just hiding from one another."

"When we leave, you'll come with us," says Mark.

I look at Mark. Of course, it's the right thing to do. I'm sure we were all thinking it, but we waited for Mark to say it.

Bill shakes his head. "No, I don't want to be a burden."

I stare at the veins on Bill's hands. "We need to take you with us. You can't stay here."

Bill looks at me with tears in his eyes. I go over to him and give him a hug. "It will be good, Bill. You'll see."

***

After we've eaten our food, we clean up and relax. Sara is no longer sitting in the chair. She's in her sleeping bag. I think about the time when the zombie almost got her. I notice blood from that zombie still stains her bag. I cross my fingers that Sara will be better in the morning.

***

Bill is resting on one of the beds. I'm glad we were able to feed him, and I'm sure he prefers sleeping on a bed to sleeping in a bathtub.

Gary is sleeping next to him. Katie has the other bed to herself, for now. Sara is in her sleeping bag on the floor.

It's no surprise that I'm still awake, but so is Mark. We're sitting at a table, our space lit with candles.

"I'm glad we convinced Bill to come with us."

"Of course; we can't leave him here."

I kiss Mark on the lips. Then I look over at Gary to make sure he's still asleep. The last thing I need is for him to wake up and be staring at us.

Then Mark kisses me on the lips, allowing me to melt into his mouth, once again.

But then Mark pulls his lips away and puts his hands on my head. "I wish I could kiss you all night, but we should get some sleep, yeah?"

"I'd like to sleep with you." I'm surprised at myself for blurting it out.

Mark raises his eyebrow. "Well, I could take you into the bathroom and lay you in the bathtub."

I laugh, grateful Mark is going with it. "No, I don't think Bill would appreciate us doing it in his bathroom."

Mark kisses me on the lips again. "Someday, Jen, someday soon, I hope. Now let's go get some sleep."

I nod my head. Instead of sleeping next to Katie, I decide to place my sleeping bag on the floor next to Mark's. We lie side by side. Mark holds my hand as I fall asleep.

16.

I FEEL A TAP ON MY BACK. I look up. Katie is standing over me. "Have you seen Sara?"

"No, Katie. I've been asleep." I look over at Sara's empty sleeping bag. "Did you check the bathroom?"

Katie rolls her eyes. "Yes. She's not here."

Bill is sitting up in his bed, but Gary is still sleeping. "Did she run away?" Bill asks.

"I don't know!" I say as I rush out of my sleeping bag.

"What's the matter?" says Mark, waking up.

"Sara's not here."

"Christ! Okay, let's go find her."

"I'm coming with you," I say.

"What's going on?" says Gary, waking up as well.

"Sara's gone," says Mark. "We've got to find her."

"You guys stay put," I tell Bill and Katie. "We'll go out and look for her."

* * *

Gary, Mark, and I check the van, but there's no Sara. There is a parking lot in front of the motel, a road, and then woods next to the road. "Let's go look in the woods. Maybe she's in there," I say.

"She could be any fucking where," says Gary. "This is bullshit!"

"Gary, stop making it worse," I say.

"Yeah," says Mark. "Let's just find her."

I want to scream Sara's name, but I know that's not the thing to do anymore if you've lost someone. You can attract zombies by screaming, just like you can attract them with gunshots.

We walk into the woods, guns ready, leaves and twigs bunching and crackling under our shoes. My nerves are on high alert. I know there are zombies in here.

It doesn't take me long to see it. Everyone knows Sara by her black boots. They're sticking out from behind a tree.

I grab Mark's arm. He looks at me. Then I point at the tree. Mark motions to Gary and we all rush over. I gasp. Sure enough, just as I feared, there's Sara, on her back behind the tree. Her arms are stretched above her, her gun by her arms.

I look at her head. Blood covers the ground below it. Her hair and her face are also covered with blood. I fall into Mark's arms and he holds me tight.

"Damn, Sara, why'd you do it?" says Gary.

I cry as Mark pulls me in tighter and then I feel Gary coming in to hug as well. We all just hold each other, in silence, as Sara's body lies by our feet.

Then, we hear them. Zombies coming our way. There aren't three or four or even ten. We see twenty or thirty.

"Oh my God," I say. "We've got to move Sara."

"No! There are too many. Run!" says Gary.

"Come on, Jen. Let's move!" says Mark.

We run out of the woods. I don't look back. I can't look back.

We bang the motel room's door, and Bill lets us in. Then I fall on a bed, unable to move or breathe. We've lost three people to this horrible mess. I don't think I can take losing any more.

"Where's Sara?" screams Katie.

"She's dead," says Gary.

Katie starts to cry and falls next to me on the bed. We hold each other tight.

17.

WE'RE BACK ON THE ROAD. Mark is driving and I'm up front with him, but we're not speaking. Nobody in the van is.

It doesn't surprise me that Sara took her own life. I imagine we've all felt like killing ourselves. Depression can ruin a person's body and soul, especially if the person is as fragile as Sara was.

I look behind me at Bill. He's sitting back, relaxed, writing in a crossword puzzle. We've just met him, but I know the situation we're all in has gotten to him as well. Yet, he seems to be doing what he can to calm his nerves.

Katie has never been one to hide her emotions. She's been crying most of the trip. I don't blame her.

But it's Gary who has changed. Now he's calm, quiet, a man beaten by all this, whether he has admitted it to himself or not. His callous attitude and grins are gone, and he looks human.

Mark pulls the van over to the side of the road so we can pee. I don't need to go and neither does Katie. Mark, Bill, and Gary pee and then after Gary finishes, he leans against the side of the van to smoke a cigarette.

I leave the van to go talk to him. "Hi."

"Hey," he says.

"How are you?"

"I'm good." He doesn't look at me.

I bump him. "You sure about that?"

This time, Gary does look at me. He tries to smile, but then he brings a finger to his eye and wipes it. "It's crazy, you know? It just goes on and on."

"Yeah, I know." Tears well in my eyes as well. "Just think about Texas and how great it's gonna be over there."

"He's got you buying that shit too, huh?"

I'm not mad at Gary for saying it. I've tried not to question Mark's plan, but my skepticism is still there. "Well, I have to hope the place is gonna be okay. Otherwise, I guess we'll have to go find a camp to live in."

"Nah, screw that."

"Yeah, I guess the camps are not the best places to be."

"I lived in one for a month, over in Indiana." He looks at me. "You ever been to prison?"

I laugh. "No."

"A camp is just another prison. Just another overcrowded prison."

"They seem scary to me."

"A girl like you would have a hard time there." Gary looks me up and down. "Yeah, that's for sure."

I hate when Gary inspects me, but I'm trying hard to like him.

"No, once we get to Texas, I'll go out on my own. Go find me someplace to hole up and some woman to hole up with."

I laugh. "You got it all figured out, huh?"

"You gonna stay with Mark? Be his woman?"

You'd have to be blind not to know that Mark and I like each other. "Yeah, I'm staying with Mark."

"So what you gonna do with dipshit and the old man?" Gary takes another smoke. "'Cause they're not coming with me."

"Katie and Bill can stay with Mark and me. Lord knows Katie can't make it on her own. I would hate for anything to happen to her. And obviously, Bill needs us as well."

Mark walks over to Gary and me. "You folks ready? We need to get moving."

"Yep, we're ready." It occurs to me that the entire time I'm talking to Gary, I don't even think about zombies. Even though I question how safe Mark's home is in Texas, it's become a huge fantasy for me to think the place is secure enough for a person to de-stress in all this.

I never thought I would spend my life with someone like Katie or that Bill would come into my life, but we all need one another now. Gary thinks about Gary and that's no surprise, but I do hope that if he decides to go on his own, he'll be okay.

18.

WE'VE FOUND ANOTHER ABANDONED HOME, a ranch that looks to be less than ten years old.

The neighborhood it's in reminds me of Waterbank, the small, quiet place where I grew up. Yet, unlike what I left in Waterbank, I'm not staring at dead bodies here.

Green signs are on the doors of these homes, directing people to a nearby camp.

Many people have abandoned their houses for these camps. The government encouraged people to do it.

I've never thought the government has people's best interests in mind. It's ironic that I'm now living with people who feel the same.

It wasn't hard for Gary and Mark to break into the house, and now they're checking it out.

Me? I'm sitting here with a knot in my stomach, content just to wait in the van with Katie and Bill. I have no interest in proving my worth as a female in the zombie apocalypse. It's natural for Mark to take over and to call on a fellow male for help. That's just the way he is. I don't feel the need to prove anything to him or to anyone right now.

I sit next to Katie. I put my arm around her, and she looks at me with those bright blue eyes. Then, she puts her head on my shoulder. The energy has left her usual bubbly self.

* * *

As I'm looking at the house, I see a zombie walk out the front door. Judging by the tattered and dirty skirt it wears, the zombie looks like it was once a female. Half its head is missing, as if some other zombie took a chomp out of it when it was human.

The knot in my stomach tightens. Are Mark and Gary okay?

The zombie heads straight for the van. It doesn't seem to see us, but it's coming for us. Then, the zombie veers off to the left and wanders off.

I look at Katie and Bill. "You guys duck down. I've gotta go see if Mark and Gary are okay."

Holding my machete, I get off the van and run to the front door.

Slowly, I walk inside the house. Mark and Gary come downstairs. "Jen?" says Mark.

"Yeah, I saw a zombie walk out the door. So I came in here to make sure you and Gary were cool."

"I thought we closed the door, but it's obviously a good thing we didn't," says Mark. "While we were upstairs, we heard something moving around, but we never found it. The zombie you saw leaving the house must have been it. There are no other zombies in the house. So let's get Bill and Katie out of van now."

As we head back outside, I see that the same zombie I saw leaving the house has got its hands on one of the windows of the van, growling and trying to get to the humans inside. Katie and Bill are still ducked down, but one of them must have gotten up at some point

I run to the zombie with my machete. It immediately turns to look at me, and it growls with that sound that will haunt me for as long as I live, coming after me, hands sprawled. I plunge the machete into the part of its head that still exists. Blood splatters and, as it falls on me, I manage to roll out from under it.

Then, even though the zombie is down and permanently disabled, Gary rushes up to it and shoots it in the head. "Cocksucker!" he says.

Mark rushes over to me. "Hey! Good job!"

"Thanks. We better go check on Bill and Katie."

Gary, Mark, and I enter the van. Bill is still crouched down in his seat. I don't think he's moved since I asked him to duck. But Katie has changed seats. She stares at me with saucer blue eyes. "I thought it was gonna get us."

"Well, it's dead now," I say. "Let's go get in the house. It's safe there."

19.

THE SALT AND PEPPER SHAKERS in the kitchen of this house are little black and white cows. My mother would have loved these.

She decorated our home in country modern with colorful pillows and quilts and her beloved cow collection.

I think about my mother and how much I miss her. When she died, we were not close, but I had hoped someday that would change.

"You okay?" Mark says to me.

I look at him with tears in my eyes. "I'm fine. I just miss my mom, is all." Mark puts his arms around me and hugs me tight.

Inside the kitchen cupboards and pantry, we've managed to find food supplies we can use. We can add the items to our stash.

Katie, Bill, Gary, and I have decided to sleep in the bedrooms rather than sleep in our sleeping bags. I'm staying with Katie in one bedroom. Gary and Bill are in another. However, Mark has decided to sleep in his sleeping bag in the living room by the front door, where he can keep his eyes and ears peeled for anything.

The worst thing about staying in an abandoned home are the family photos I see. In this house, it looks like there were two girls and three boys, plus the parents. They look at the camera, happy and not knowing a zombie apocalypse was coming. Are they all alive and living at a camp? I hope the zombie who wandered out of here was not the mother.

20.

"YOU KNOW THAT CONVENIENCE STORE WE PASSED ON THE WAY HERE?" Gary says to me.

"Yeah."

"Let's go check it out. Maybe there will be cigarettes."

"You've got a million cigarettes, Gary. Seriously?"

"Let's go check it out."

I sigh. "I'll wake Mark up and . . ."

"Let the dude sleep. It's just up the street. Katie and Bill can stay here too."

"Okay, you're right. Sounds like a plan. Let me get my rifle. Do you want me to drive?"

Gary holds up the keys. "No, I got it."

* * *

As Gary and I leave the house to enter the van, I look around for zombies. I don't see any, but I know they're out here.

No sooner do we get on the road, a zombie wanders onto it. It's young and thin with long, dirty auburn hair, and it's wearing a ragged shirt and torn blue jeans. I get a sick feeling looking at it, not just because it's a zombie, but because it's my look-alike. It's what I could become.

It stares at nothing in particular as it enters the road, but then it sees us and its expression changes to a rabid undead after its prey.

"Watch this," says Gary.

"What are you going to do?"

Gary drives up to the zombie. Much closer than I want him to.

Then Gary puts his gun up to the zombie's face as it approaches, and shoots. The zombie's head splits open and the blood splatters all over Gary's clothes, and a bit of it lands on me as well.

"Gary! What the hell?"

"That was awesome!"

"Look at you. It's all on you. Let's just get to the store."

* * *

We're approaching the store. From the outside, it appears ransacked. Still, it's worth looking inside.

"Okay, get ready to roll," I say. But Gary gives me the meanest look I have ever seen and just keeps on driving.

"What are you doing? The store is back there."

* * *

I open my eyes. My upper body is lying on the seat behind Gary. My head feels like it's been hit with a baseball bat. My hands are tied behind my back and there's duct tape over my mouth. I sit up.

"Back down, bitch, before I kill you," Gary screams.

I put my head back on the seat. I'm shaking and my heart is thumping. What's going on? Why did Gary do this to me? What's going to happen to me?

It's not just my head that hurts; my nose and mouth, covered in duct tape, feel as though they've been smacked as well. I lie quiet, wondering how far Gary has driven past the store.

The car is moving, but not too fast. It seems Gary has driven off the main path and onto a side road. I look up at the window and watch the trees pass. Then I look over to the side door.

If I can get to it, my hands are free enough to manipulate the handle. Maybe I can pull it open and get out. I'm thankful Gary didn't tie my feet as well.

Gary swerves the car. "Fuck," he screams. The car veers off the road and then it stops, almost crashing into some trees. Two zombies throw themselves at Gary's partly open window.

As Gary shoots one in the head, I move my body over to the side door and struggle with the handle. I pull open the door enough for me to squeeze out. Then I run, duct tape over my mouth and hands tied behind my back.

I dash through the trees, but then I trip, and my face falls hard against the ground. The pain is excruciating as I roll to my knees and get back to my feet. If zombies are around, I don't notice. If they are chasing me, I don't know.

But I heard Gary peel the van off the road and leave. I know he hasn't come after me. He's left me out here, bound, mouth covered in duct tape, and no weapon to protect me.

21.

I PLOP DOWN BY A TREE. My head jerks around, looking in every direction for zombies, and then I see it: a house and a woman standing near it, holding a gun and looking around her.

I lift myself up from the ground and then I run to her. When she sees me, her eyes grow big. Rather than help me, she runs inside the house and slams the door.

I keep running toward the house. My hands are tied behind my back, but my plan is to kick the door. I can't let this woman ignore me.

I reach the home. I notice a weathered and torn American flag has flown off of its holder and lays by a pot of dead flowers. On the door is a sign: *The Finn Family.*

I see two zombies in the distance. They don't see me. But if I don't get help soon, they will. I kick the door.

The windows of the house are boarded up, but one window is not completely covered, and I can see a curtain behind the wood. The curtain opens and then shuts fast. Is the woman scared of me? Does she think I'm a zombie? Why won't she let me inside? Doesn't she realize I need help?

Now the zombies see me, and they're headed my way. I kick the door again. This time the door opens. A man answers, holding a gun in his hand. I hear zombie growls. He pulls me into the house, then I hear gunshots, and the growls stop. The man slams the door.

"Over here; please sit down," says the man. The woman who ran away from me is there as well. A little girl, who looks to be about five or six, stands by her side.

I take a seat in a chair, holding my tied arms to the side. The man gently removes the duct tape from my mouth. Tears roll down my face.

"Thank you," I say.

"Let me untie you," says the man. "My goodness, what happened to you?"

"What happened to her, Daddy?" says the little girl.

"Go to your room," says the woman. The little girl runs away.

"Someone whom I thought was a friend hit me and knocked me out. I woke up with duct tape over my mouth and my hands tied. I managed to escape before he could do anything further to me." As the rope leaves my wrists, I rub them.

"You say this was a friend?" says the woman. "What friend would do this?"

"I've been traveling with a group of people. I went on a supply run with one of them in our van. We were going to check out a store we saw. Then, before I knew it, he knocked me unconscious."

"But where is this person," says the woman. "Are we in danger?"

"No. He drove off. We're safe here."

"I'm Joe," says the man. "This is my wife, Linda, and our daughter's name is Carrie."

"Hello," I say.

"Your face is bruised. I don't have ice," says Linda. "But would you like some water? I can bring you a cloth for your face."

"Yes, thank you."

Without smiling and with the same blank expression, Linda leaves the room.

I look at Joe. "I don't know what I would have done if I had not found this house."

"I'm glad you got my attention," says Joe. "We've been locked in here, and so far, we've been fine. Those two zombies I just shot were only the fourth and fifth zombies I've put down since we've been shut inside. Not many out there."

As Joe talks, I can't help but think about Gary. He hit me, took me away from everyone. What about the others? Will he hurt them? Will he go after Mark? Suddenly, severe panic overtakes me and I start to cry.

"Now, don't worry," says Joe. "You're here now. You can stay here until we can get you back to your folks."

"But, we were traveling to Texas and just passing through. I don't know where I am. Gary, the guy who hurt me, left me here because he knew nobody would be able to find me."

"I see."

Linda returns with a bottle of water and a washcloth.

"Thank you." I take a sip of the water.

"Are you staying?" she asks.

"Yes, of course she's staying, dear," says Joe. "It's getting dark."

"Fine. I'll set another plate." Linda leaves the room again. I spread the wet washcloth over my face. I can tell Gary banged me up pretty good.

"I'm worried sick about my boyfriend and the rest of my friends. Gary may go for them."

"You'll have to put your worries aside for tonight. We'll go looking for them in the morning. You said you were headed to a store? Are your friends staying close to the store?"

"Yes, but I have no idea how far it is from here. I think the store was called Red Robin, or something."

"Sounds familiar. We'll find it. I know these parts well."

22.

STANDING IN THE FINN'S BATHROOM, I'm shocked at what I see in the mirror. A large bruise extends from my forehead, down one side of my face. I have a black eye and a busted lip. I don't know how many times Gary hit me.

I leave the bathroom and head to where I hear conversations. In the kitchen, lighted with oil lamps, are four plates of food on the kitchen table.

"Please, come sit down," says Joe.

"Thanks!"

"What happened to you?" asks Carrie. She's got strawberry blonde hair and freckles on her face, like her mother.

"Hush. That's none of your business," says Linda.

I respect Linda's wishes, and I'm not sure how I could explain to someone so young what happened to me.

I pick up my fork to eat. Joe says, "Now it's time for the blessing." I put my fork down.

"Gracious Lord, we thank you for this food that we're about to receive, in the nourishment of our bodies, for Christ sake, amen," says Joe.

"Amen," I say, feeling a bit like a faker. My family never said prayers.

"After we eat, we'll show you where you can sleep for the night," says Joe. "In the morning, we'll go look for your friends."

I nod my head, grateful for the food and for finding a safe place to escape zombies and Gary.

* * *

After dinner, Linda takes me to the bedroom where I will sleep. She gives me a toothbrush, a flashlight, and a nightgown. The gown is pink with flowers on it, something I would never wear, but I'm not complaining.

I pull back the covers of the twin bed and climb inside. Then I stare up at the ceiling. I'm still worried sick about Mark and the others. I'm assuming Gary went back to the house after he left me. Or, maybe he just took off with the van. The van has all our supplies, but at least everyone would be safe.

As I'm lying in bed, in walks Carrie. She carries a flashlight and a worn stuffed bear.

"Do you live here now?" she asks.

"No, no. I'm just staying here for the night. Aren't you supposed to be asleep? It's late."

Without answering me, she climbs in the bed. The light from the flashlight helps her see my bruises. "What happened to your face?"

I pause for a moment. "Some guy was mean to me, but that's all over now."

"Oh."

"Carrie, get to bed!" Linda is standing at the door, holding a flashlight too.

Carrie gives me a hug and then runs out the room. "Is there anything you need?" Linda asks.

"No, I'm fine. Thanks."

"You're welcome. Goodnight." Linda walks away. I'm not sure why, but Linda doesn't seem to like me much.

* * *

I can't believe I've slept through the night. I didn't dream about zombies. I didn't wake up in the middle of the night soaked in sweat. I slept more than I've slept in a long time.

I climb out of bed, wearing the pink nightgown, and go to the bathroom. The Finns have a composting toilet, perfect for the situation we're in. They seem prepared for the way the U.S. has become.

I stare into the bathroom mirror. My face looks worse, but I know the bruises are healing.

I smooth my hair back, and then, with bottled water, I wipe my face and brush my teeth.

Then I go into the kitchen. Linda, dressed for the day, is making coffee with a portable coffee maker. She turns to look at me. "Good morning. Would you like a cup?"

I smile. "Yes." It's been a long time since I've had a hot cup of coffee.

I take a seat. Linda is smiling a little. I've never seen her smile.

"I'm happy you're up, because I wanted to chat with you for a bit," says Linda.

"Okay."

Linda looks around the room. "Joe and I have been in this house for twenty years. I never want to leave it."

I take a sip of my coffee. "It's a nice house. Seems really comfortable."

"It's not big, but I've made it into a comfortable home for me and my family."

"How long have you and Joe been married?"

"Eighteen years. I thought I would lose him the first time he had to fight off a zombie, but he's been able to protect himself, and us."

"I always wanted to get married, but I don't know if that will ever happen for me. The world is crazy right now. I just want to stay alive. That's all I can think about."

"Yes, the world has changed. But what you have to understand about Joe and me is that we are happy. Despite this, we are happy, and I will do everything in my power to protect our happiness, because things weren't always good between Joe and me."

"No?"

"No. Before the zombies, Joe had girlfriends and he was addicted to porn."

I look away. I don't need to hear about Joe's porn addiction.

"I'm sorry if I'm embarrassing you, but now that we don't have Internet and there are zombies everywhere, Joe has had to change his ways." Linda puts down her cup. "You're a very pretty girl, Jennifer. You're just the sort of girl Joe is attracted to."

"Oh, Linda, don't worry about me. I would never do anything."

"Yes, I know you would never do anything. But, I can't say the same thing about Joe. Please do whatever you can to find your friends."

"Yes, I plan on it."

"Because I don't want you back here, and if you do come back, I'm going to make it very difficult for you here."

I look at Linda, shocked at what I'm hearing. "I'm sorry you feel this way about me, but I would never do anything."

"I don't mean to be rude, but zombies are the best thing that could have happened to my relationship with Joe. I have the marriage and family I want. It's been hard on Carrie, but she'll survive."

I place my coffee cup on the counter and force a smile. "Okay, well, thanks for letting me know and thanks for the coffee. I'm going to get dressed now." I walk out of the kitchen.

Joe is standing in the hallway. "Good morning. Are you ready to find your folks soon?"

"Yes," I say to Joe. "More than ready."

* * *

I've changed back into my clothes and I'm ready to go. Linda gives Joe a hug. "Be careful out there," she says to him.

"I will. Don't worry."

"I wish you didn't have to do this. But I realize there's no other way. We need to get this girl back to her friends." Linda looks at me. "Jennifer, it was nice meeting you. Now, I've got some things to do before Carrie wakes up."

"It was nice meeting you too, and please tell Carrie I said goodbye. She's such a sweet little girl."

Linda smiles and then she leaves the room. I've thought about what she told me in the kitchen. There's no way I'm coming back here.

23.

THE ZOMBIES JOE SHOT when I arrived here are no longer lying in front of his house. Joe says he buries any zombies he kills on his property. He says every zombie was a human and humans deserve respectable resting places.

Joe owns a red pick-up truck, splattered with dirt. He is tall with thick dark hair and a dark mustache. Even though I figure he's a lot older than I am, he's handsome for his age, and he has a kind smile. Although what Linda told me shocked me, I can understand why she wants to protect her household. I can see why women would be attracted to Joe and I can see how he can get women attracted to him.

I get inside Joe's truck. "Fasten your seat belt, please," says Joe.

"Sure," I say. "Thank you, again, for doing this for me. I'm worried sick about my friends."

"The store you and that fella were headed to is one I've been to before." Joe grips the steering wheel. "We can drive to it and then maybe you'll remember how to get to your friends."

"Sounds good." I look down at the handgun inside the holster on Joe's waist. "My rifle was in the van when Gary took off with it. I don't know if I'll ever see it again. My dad gave it to me."

"Maybe you will see it again. In the meantime, there's a gun in the glove compartment. It's loaded. It's there if we need it."

"Thanks."

"How did you get hooked up with this Gary in the first place?"

"I met him and a bunch of other people back in Illinois. They were living in a garage. The funny thing is, Gary is the one who saved me from a zombie. He shot it."

Joe looks at me. "Well, he attacked you pretty good, but you'll heal soon enough."

"Yeah, thank goodness." By my feet is an old straw that looks like it came from a fast food restaurant. It's a reminder of my old life and of the things I may never see again.

"Look out!" says Joe. On the road in front of us is a large crowd of zombies. There is no room for the truck to pass.

I reach for the gun in the glove compartment. "Oh my God, this doesn't look good."

Joe picks up speed as we approach the zombies. He hits one and it falls to the ground. Then another zombie jumps on the truck. Joe swerves the truck, and the zombie falls off. In the process, he hits another zombie, but we make our way out.

I sit stunned in my seat. "God, I hope we don't run into more."

"You just never know."

I take a few deep breaths to calm myself and shake my head on how fucked up the world is. I didn't think everything would go to hell during my lifetime.

* * *

Heading toward us is a blue car. It's one of the few cars I've seen on the road here. The car passes me and the guy inside the car looks at me. To my surprise, it's Mark.

"Joe, stop the truck!"

Mark stops the car he's driving. I run out of the truck as Mark runs toward me. As soon as our bodies meet, we hug each other tight. Then we kiss each other hard on the lips.

"You're safe. Thank God, you're safe," says Mark.

"You're okay." Tears roll down my face.

Joe walks up to us, smiling. "So this must be your boyfriend?"

"Yes, oh my God, Joe. This is my Mark."

"It's nice to meet you, sir." Mark offers his hand. "Thank you for helping Jen."

"We ran into a bit of a zombie snag, but we survived it," says Joe. "You folks will be okay, then?"

"Yes, Joe. Thank you so, so much."

"No problem! I'm going to take a different route home. Don't want to face that crowd of zombies again."

"Good idea," I say. I give Joe a hug.

"You stay away from Gary," says Joe.

"She'll never have to worry about that guy again," says Mark.

"Good. All right. Take care." Joe gets back in his truck and drives off.

Mark and I walk back to the car. While we're walking, we're holding onto each other tightly. Mark looks at my face. "What in the hell did he do to you?"

We get inside the car. I cry hard, grabbing Mark.

Then Mark pulls me from him and looks at me. "What did he do to you, Jen? Tell me?"

"He knocked me out, and then, after I woke up, I saw he had tied my hands behind my back and put duct tape on my mouth."

"Jesus Christ!"

"Mark, at least he didn't rape me or something. You said I don't have to worry about him anymore . . . did you kill him?"

"No, I didn't kill him. I wanted to kill him, but I didn't. Katie and Bill told me you went to the store. So I waited for you to return. But Gary was the only one who came back. He told us zombies attacked you and you were dead."

Mark holds me tight again. "I didn't believe his story for one second, though. I've always been able to read Gary. He twitches his eye when he lies. I raced out right after he claimed you were dead."

"I managed to get the van's door open and I ran out. Gary didn't come for me. He just left me in the woods. I guess given the monster he is, that's a good thing. But if it wasn't for Joe and his family, I don't know what would have happened to me. Where did you find this car?"

"It was parked in the back of the house. It had gas in it too. I found the keys hanging up in the kitchen."

"When did you go looking for me? Were you out all night?"

"Yeah. When it got dark, I parked the car on the side of the road, hid myself under this blanket in the back seat over there, and slept."

"I didn't die. Gary didn't win. But Gary is with Bill and Katie. Do you think they're safe?"

"All I wanted to do was find you, and that meant leaving everyone back at the house. But now, we need to get back. We'll get Katie and Bill, and we'll leave. Gary is on his own."

"I'm scared. I'm scared to face him."

"I'm here with you now, Jen. We'll face the prick together."

I've been trying to be brave through all this, but that's with zombies. With a human, a sick human, I need Mark with me, even though I know he can't protect me every time some mean guy tries to hurt me.

Mark looks me in the eyes, and once again, he kisses me on the lips. We push into each other, our tongues intertwined. I wish I could kiss Mark forever.

Then we hear a growl. A zombie is coming for us and its close. Mark's window is open, and there's no time to start the car.

As the zombie approaches the car, Mark shoots the zombie. He misses its head, but then he shoots several more times until he hits his target. The zombie falls to the ground and Mark starts the car. We pull off.

"I love you," says Mark.

"I love you too."

"We're gonna get back to the house, grab Katie and Bill, and then get the hell out of here."

"You're sure you know the way back?"

"Yeah, I'm sure." Mark looks at me. "Man, he hit you hard, didn't he?"

"I'm okay. It's healing."

"I'm so fucking mad."

I'm not used to Mark swearing, and I don't think I've ever seen him this angry. The sky is cloudy. I watch the raindrops on the window. A zombie shuffles along the road, watching our car pass.

24.

WE MAKE IT BACK TO THE HOUSE and, when we do, two zombies are on the front lawn. Mark doesn't miss a beat. He rushes out and shoots at both of them until they're down.

I'm still in the car. "Jen, come on!"

Butterflies take over my stomach. It's not zombies I'm afraid of, right now. It's Gary. If he's in the house, what can we expect from him?

* * *

Inside, Katie runs up to me and gives me a hug. "Jennifer, you're alive!"

"Yes, Gary said you were dead," says Bill.

I hug Katie back. "Well, Gary is wrong. Where is he?"

"Do you know what he did?" says Katie. "He took the van and went off with it. That was hours ago."

"What?!" says Mark.

"Yeah, it occurred to me I didn't see the van out front," I say.

"He said you'll never see him again," says Katie. "He's such an asshole. Let's go find him and get our van back."

"We can't do that," says Mark. "We don't have enough gas to do that."

"What do you suggest?" I ask.

"We should wait and see if Gary has a change of heart. If he's not back by tomorrow, we leave in the car."

"What happened to you out there, Jennifer?" asks Katie. "Your face looks horrible."

"Gary knocked me out, tied me up, put duct tape over my mouth. I escaped before he could do anything else to me. A family rescued me and put me up for the night."

Katie and Bill look shocked. "We should have gone with you, Jennifer," says Bill. "Maybe Gary would not have tried anything if we had been with you."

"Let's not worry about it," I say. "It could have gone worse. He could have tried to hurt everyone if we had all been in the van."

"Was he going to rape you?" says Katie.

"I don't know. But if that was his intention, I'm not surprised."

* * *

It's around five p.m. Mark and I arrived back at the house this morning at around ten a.m. During the time that Mark and I have been back at the house, Gary has not shown up. He's probably gone for good.

The van has our supplies. Without it, we're starting from scratch. Just as important, we have no extra gas for the car.

I look around for Mark. He's standing in the home's fenced-in backyard. The fence is high enough for zombies not to look in. I walk up to him and put my hand on his back.

"I don't think that douche is gonna come back," says Mark.

"Yeah, I know."

"I say we eat dinner and then get ready to head out in the morning."

"Mark, how are we going to make it with just the car? What about the gas situation?"

Mark doesn't say anything.

"I think we should think about staying here."

"Forget it, Jen. I can't . . . I can't stay here."

"I know your heart is set on Texas, but let's be smart about this."

"We'll go as far as we can in the car. Then we'll have to make it on foot."

"Make it on foot with an old man? Come on, Mark."

Mark looks at me and then he walks back in the house. I stand by myself in the backyard. I've never seen him so annoyed before. But he's going to have to face reality. I walk back in the house and re-join him.

"I want to forget about all this, you know?" Mark says.

"I know."

He pulls me in close. "Will you sleep with me tonight?"

The smile on my face does nothing to betray my thoughts. "Yes, I'd love to."

25.

THE DOOR IS LOCKED and Mark and I are naked in bed in one of the bedrooms. I've lost weight since this whole thing started, weight I didn't need to lose. I feel scrawny. But when Mark looked at my body, he told me I was beautiful.

How does Mark look? He's lovely. Why are some men's bodies so perfect looking? Not a scratch, not a stretch mark, nothing flabby, nothing.

He's kissing my neck while he places his hand on my breast. I wrap my arms around him tight. I'm wet, and I haven't been this wet in a long time.

I've had boyfriends in the past, but none made me feel the way Mark makes me feel now.

I reach for his penis, hard against my hand. I don't have birth control, and I'm smart enough not to get myself into a situation I'll regret.

This is the zombie apocalypse and there is no room for a baby in this world. But I so want for him to enter me. He puts his fingers between my legs and fondles me.

"I wish we could . . ."

"I know," he whispers.

"I want you in my mouth." Before he can say another word, I roll him on his back and hang over him. He has a smile on his face in anticipation of what I'm about to do.

As I move his penis in and out of my mouth, it doesn't take long for him to, as I like to say, "Explode." There are girls who hate to give guys head, but I'm not one of them.

* * *

In the morning, I open my eyes. Mark is lying next to me, asleep. For another night, I've slept all the way through it. Last night was so wonderful; all thoughts of zombies and Gary were gone.

But now, they're back. I feel sick knowing that Gary probably won't return. How are we going to get to Texas?

I leave the bed, put on my clothes, and walk to the living room. Bill joins me.

"Good morning."

"Good morning. Gary never came back," says Bill.

"Nope. He never did."

"I look forward to Texas."

I look at Bill. "The car won't last us long. We'll run out of gas. We may have to walk the rest of the way."

"Mark doesn't want to stay here," says Bill.

"Yes, I know."

"And neither do I. The way he describes his ranch, I would like to settle there."

"Bill, what if something bad has happened to Mark's place?"

"That's a chance we'll have to take. I think it's worth it. Don't you?"

I grin. "Yes, I guess I do."

"Good morning, all." Mark enters the room.

"Good morning," says Bill. "Please excuse me while I go eat breakfast."

I walk up to Mark, wrap my arms around him, and kiss him. "Last night was nice."

"It was awesome."

"Bill and I had an interesting conversation."

"Oh?"

"He says he doesn't want to stay here either. He says he wants to hang out with you in Texas."

Mark smiles. "I wouldn't mind hanging out with Bill. He's cool."

"So let's get ready to get out of here today."

"Gary never came back."

"Nope, he didn't. But I don't want to talk about him anymore. We'll be fine without him. We'll make it."

* * *

We're searching the house for supplies to take with us. We can't pack as much as we did with the van. We can only pack as much as we can carry, because when the car runs out of gas, we'll be on foot. We've found two empty backpacks. Katie and I are searching the house, placing items inside the backpacks.

"So you two did it last night, huh?" says Katie.

"Yep. We weren't too loud, were we?" I wink at her.

"No." Katie laughs. "Mark is a nice guy. He's not an asshole like Gary. I hope something bad happens to him."

I place batteries in one of the backpacks. "I can't say I don't agree with you. He's a jerk, that's for sure."

"You can thank me for your being with Mark, you know?"

"Oh?"

"Yeah. Mark ended up in the garage only because I convinced Gary to let him come with us."

"Mark never told me that. Of course, we haven't had much time to talk."

"We were out trying to find water, just me and Gary. We were driving this old black car. It broke down pretty soon after we found it, but we got a little bit of use out of it. Anyway, there was Mark, wandering around. When he saw us in the car, he ran up to us and then asked us if he could join us. Gary told him no. He's like, 'Get the hell out of here.' But I convinced him to turn the car around."

"Wow, how did you manage that?"

"I just kept screaming at him to turn the car around. He got sick of listening to me. So he did it. It was a good thing too. Mark changed everything for us. We were a mess before Mark showed up."

"Yes, Mark is a born leader." I give Katie a hug and kiss her on the cheek. "Thank you. I appreciate what you did for him."

Katie smiles back at me. I don't want anything to ever happen to Katie. I'll do whatever I can to protect her, and I'm sure Mark feels the same way.

26.

WE'RE BACK ON THE HIGHWAY, and I'm driving. How long will it be before this car is on empty? If we last another hour, we'll be lucky. When we have to walk, hopefully someone will stop and help us. But there's no guarantee.

"Hey, our van!" screams Katie.

Sure enough, there it is. Leaving the van are two men, carrying some of our supplies to their truck.

I stop the car and we rush out. "That's our van," screams Mark. "Get away from it."

The men don't resist us. They throw the supplies they're carrying into their truck and speed off.

We rush over to the van. Gary is nowhere to be found. We've lost some supplies, but I'm holding my rifle, still loaded, just like I left it. The men didn't take it.

"Just our luck, the keys are still in the ignition," Mark says.

"All the gasoline cans are here. Had we not gotten here when we did, who knows?" I say.

I look out a window. The zombie walking in the distance is a familiar face. It's Gary, or what used to be Gary. I'm sure of it.

I run out of the van to the thing that was Gary. It comes for me, growling with tiny pupils on its big white eyes. A sick black and green liquid spurts out of its mouth. It's not decayed, but there's dried blood all over its face and shirt from the large wound on its neck. I aim my rifle at its head and shoot. It falls. I rush up to it and shoot it again, and again. I stand and stare at its demolished face.

"Jen!" screams Mark. He runs up to me and sees the zombie on the ground. "Gary?"

"Yeah."

"You did what you needed to do."

"Yep."

Mark kisses me on the cheek. "Come on; let's go."

We run back to the van, holding hands. Katie and Bill come our way.

"You two okay?" says Bill.

"Yeah, everything is fine. Nothing to see here," says Mark. "Let's get back to the van. Texas is waiting."

ABOUT THE AUTHOR

Jolie du Pré is a full-time author, editor, article writer, blogger, and monster lover.

Join her mailing list to be notified of new releases:
Eepurl.com/QS3d5

Jolie loves to hear from her readers. You can reach her at any of the following:

Facebook:
Facebook.com/joliedupreauthor

Twitter:
Twitter.com/joliedupre

Website:
JolieDuPre.com

Blog:
PreciousMonsters.com

Email:
joliedupre@gmail.com

Thank you for reading *Benton: A Zombie Novel, Volume One*. Would you please leave a two or three sentence review on Amazon? Thanks!

Look for *Benton: A Zombie Novel, Volume Two* in July 2014.

Made in the USA
Charleston, SC
02 June 2014